Another Form

PATERSONS IN MISSOURI

David Carlyle

Another Form
Patersons in Missouri
v2.0

Outskirts Press, Inc.
http://www.outskirtspress.com

ISBN: 978-1-4787-0331-0

Library of Congress Control Number: 2013910256

Outskirts Press and the "OP" logo are trademarks belonging to Outskirts Press, Inc.

PRINTED IN THE UNITED STATES OF AMERICA

Prologue

Another Form is the second book in a four-generation, two-book saga. The story of Erroll and Kenzie Paterson continues when they step off a ship in New York in the year 1912; their return to New York completes a round trip started 25 years earlier. Erroll's father, John, had taken the children to Scotland so he could accept a job he believed better than his US job, after he ran out of money when his wife died in childbirth, and after Kenzie's mother abandoned her to him.

The Patersons endure poverty, intrigue, and physical danger at high intensity before they decide to return to the US, and at near-impossible intensity after they buy a seller-financed farm in Missouri from a traveling salesman. They travel more than 120 miles to a Scottish port, and are pursued by a rifle-toting, would-be Kenzie lover, the son of a murderous imposter. Mr. and Mrs. Ed McDowell and two families of Bradleys provide essential help during their walk, and a food wagon from Tiny Kirk in Inverness helped them before the walk.

Their poverty continues in the US for a time, as they learn shocking details about Kenzie's mother, their pursuer, the imposter, and their capacity to help people left behind.

Chapter 1
1912

Erroll and Kenzie walked near the middle of the group getting off, when their ship from Glasgow Port arrived in New York. They stepped off the pier onto US land, Erroll looked triumphantly at Kenzie, and exclaimed, "We're back, Kenzie! We're back!"

Kenzie tightened her grip on Erroll and said, "I'm going to kiss you now, Erroll." He didn't react to her kiss for the first time in his life.

They enjoyed the return to their native land and engaged in a short celebration, but only a short one. They knew they had no money, but they didn't know where to go or what to do. They expected to soon suffer and stink; exuberant Kenzie became befuddled Kenzie, when Erroll asked, "What do we do now?"

"I have no idea, Erroll." But then befuddled Kenzie became instructor and interrogator. "We find our train if it exists . . . you have the tickets. Don't you know?"

"The tickets are in my pocket, still in the jar you put them in. I'll get them, but we need to know where to find the train, Kenzie. Maybe directions are written on the tickets." He fumbled in his pocket, pulled out the jar, and found the tickets inside it. His eyes scanned words on a ticket. "It says something about Chicago—"

"You're a great woodsman, Erroll, but you know nothing about cities. We're in New York, not Chicago. We have several train tickets and you're looking at the wrong one."

"Maybe. But this ticket also has 'New York' written on it. Perhaps it's for a ride from here to there . . . to Chicago?"

"Let me look." Kenzie grabbed the ticket from Erroll and studied it. "Yes, this is a ticket we want. Do you have another like it?"

"We have two of everything, don't we? Yes, here's another one."

"You keep that one, Erroll, put the others back in the jar, and I'll keep this one. We must now suppose there's a train, board it if we can find it, and hope there really is a farm for us at the end of the ride."

"Do you know where the train is, Kenzie?"

Kenzie snapped, "Do I have to know everything for both of us?" After a pause, culminated by a frown, she added, "How can I know where a train is, that probably doesn't exist? I wonder how we can find out? We'll never know if there really is a farm in 'Missouri,' or wherever, unless the tickets are real, and there's a train somewhere."

"Do you have a safe pocket for your ticket, Kenzie?"

"Yes, I—"

"I see a bunch of people lined up to go past that counter over there, Kenzie. They're showing papers to the man wearing a uniform. Maybe he knows where a train is."

She frowned again. "Perhaps. Let's rest here until the line's shorter." They sat on a bench for a while, and Erroll found their UK/US citizenship papers. They entered the line and showed the papers to the uniformed man. He pronounced the papers fine, and said they could go on.

Erroll didn't move on when the man permitted it, but inquired about his train ticket. The man replied, "Let me see it."

Erroll handed the ticket to the man, he glanced at it, and advised, "You want Penn Station." He gave the ticket back to Erroll, looked at the couple behind them in line, and called, "Next."

Erroll tried to learn more. "Can you tell me where Penn Station is, Sir?"

"Can't you see I got a job here? Keep moving."

"But I'm new here, Sir, I don't—"

"I got no time for you. Move on."

Erroll turned to Kenzie again. "The man says we want to go to Penn Station."

"That's no help, Erroll. I don't suppose you know where Penn Station is. Gullible as you are, you probably think it exists, but we don't even know that much."

"I don't know where it is, but maybe somebody does. Let's get out of this crowd of newcomers, and try to find somebody who lives here." They heard directions to Penn Station they couldn't interpret, including, "It's in midtown," and "Over on Seventh Avenue." The best answer they received incorporated a pointed finger. "It's up that way."

They walked a long time, and Kenzie lagged behind. "Do you think we should ask again?"

"If the guy told us right about the direction, all we have to do is walk until we stumble across it."

"What if he's wrong? What if we're off by twenty degrees? Maybe we already walked past it and don't know it. I'm not convinced New York has a place called 'Penn Station,' but even if it does, we'll never find it."

"Trains make noise and smoke, Kenzie. We'll hear it or smell it if we get close."

"I'm going to ask someone, Erroll." People milled all about, and she asked the nearest person.

The lady responded, "It's that way." She pointed too, and added, "But it's at least a couple miles."

Kenzie thanked the lady, and then asked Erroll, "How many km is that?"

"I don't know, Kenzie, but a mile's bigger than a km, so it's more than two km."

They continued their walk/ask sequence, and reached a huge building labeled 'Penn Station,' about an hour after dark. They went in, asked a few more times, and found a locked ticket booth with a schedule posted on a window. According to the schedule, a train—their train—would leave for Chicago the next morning. They had no money, no food, and no prospect of food, but they were hungry. They waited on a nearby bench, because Kenzie said she supposed they couldn't camp in the vicinity.

"Did we come all this way on a wild goose chase, Erroll, merely to be lost in a huge city and probably starve to death?"

"No, Kenzie. I don't know how we'll eat, and I'm hungry too, but we'll find something. We always do."

"The stuff you find is a fruit tree in the woods, or a young rabbit you can catch. I don't think we'll see anything like that in New York. I don't know what Chicago looks like, but it could be as bad."

They waited on the bench all night, and didn't eat or sleep. They stunk up the area so much they had the bench to themselves, their stomachs growled, and their once-clean clothes showed grime when the train arrived the next day. They nevertheless boarded the train and found their assigned spot, a sleeper, scheduled to travel more than twenty-four hours to Chicago. They grinned when they saw bunks, cleaned up in a nearby restroom, and crashed into the bunks. They felt nothing except their hunger when they awoke, however.

Kenzie inquired, "How much money's in the jar?"

"I'll look." He counted five coins. "Exactly sixty pence."

Kenzie accepted the information impassively at first, but then put her hand to her head. "You know what, Erroll? I bet UK money's no good in the US. . . . we should've spent the last of it before we left."

Erroll's countenance reflected Kenzie's stricken look. "Oh, no. You're probably right. Even if you're wrong, I have no idea how much food we can buy with it, but I'm about to find out."

"Don't bother, Erroll. Nothing works out for us, ever."

"Oh, Kenzie, don't you remember the McDowells? The Bradleys, the boss's liveryman and butler back in Scotland? How can you say nothing works out for us?"

"If you can buy anything with sixty pence, I'll get down on my knees and beg your forgiveness."

"Begin to practice; I'm on the way." Erroll went out of the sleeper room and turned toward a 'Dining Car' sign, but met a man in a uniform, with a tray piled high with food.

Erroll already had the money in his hand, and offered it to the man in exchange for the food on the tray. The man said he intended to deliver the food to somebody else, but he wanted to investigate the UK money. He asked Erroll to wait until he returned, so he waited. The man took the tray into a nearby sleeper room, came back out with an older man, introduced the old guy as a coin collector, and asked Erroll to show the man his money.

The older man questioned, "What do you want for that, Son?"

He replied, "I don't know what it's worth, but you can have it all if you buy my wife and me a tray of food like you received, and you'll probably save our lives. You can't imagine how hungry we are."

The old man smiled. "What you have there is ordinary money I can go to any bank and buy at face value. It's worth sixty pence, and no more, but I don't like to think I'm on a train with hungry people. I'll bring that food and give it to you; you can keep your money."

Erroll tried to thank the man. "Mr. . . . what's your name?"

"Never mind about my name. I'll be back with the tray." The man went into his sleeper car, and came out with it. He gave it to Erroll, chuckled, and resumed, "I'm giving you the food only; the tray belongs to the railroad, and you can leave it in your car in Chicago."

Erroll accepted the tray and tried again to thank the man, but he went away almost as fast as he appeared, so Erroll turned to the man in the uniform. "Please, please tell that guy how much I appreciate this food. And I appreciate you for arranging it. Thank you. I'll try to repay you when I can. What's your name?"

The man in uniform said he just wanted to help, and then disappeared into the dining car.

Erroll went back to his own car and showed the tray to Kenzie. "Let's see you do that knee business!"

"Erroll! How did you do that?" Kenzie didn't go to her knees, but instead joined him as he ate.

Erroll crammed food in his mouth and couldn't immediately tell Kenzie how he did it, but when he could, he quipped, "I'll never tell." She didn't follow up, and he never told. They ate all the food before they stopped, but it filled them.

The train arrived at Chicago Union Station on Monday, the next day, and they went from the train into another big station. They exited their first train rested, clean, and only mildly hungry, in contrast to their condition when they boarded it. They waited another long time and didn't bother to look outside, but again sat on a bench. The title of their second train included strange city names they didn't know, the Chicago, Peoria, and St. Louis train, and they had coach seats rather than a sleeper car. They left Chicago late Monday afternoon, and arrived in St. Louis Tuesday morning. They slept in their coach car, but didn't have food, and complained about potential starvation to each other before they entered St. Louis Union Station.

Kenzie saw a sign in the station about a 'People Feeder Group,' offering food to homeless people, and pointed it out. "We must go there, Erroll. I know you don't want charity, but we're truly desperate. Do you realize it's Tuesday, and we last ate on Sunday night?"

"You might not believe it, Kenzie, but I agree with you this time. Before we go, though, we need to make sure we don't go away so long we miss our train to Rounder. We gotta learn when it goes before we do anything else." Their ticket specified a train called the MKT, and a posted schedule showed it would depart at midnight. They returned their attention to food, asked several people, and eventually found someone to tell them how to find the People Feeder Group. They walked a long way, but the walk worked out kinks after their long sit on the train.

They waited with a bunch of other people at the Group, ate, and Kenzie commented, "I loved that. Don't you think food tastes better when we're about to starve?"

"Perhaps, but maybe there's still more food, Kenzie. Some people over there have cake."

"You don't need cake, Erroll. You ate more meatloaf and potatoes than any ten men should eat!"

"I can eat more cake than any ten men should eat, too. You watch." Erroll didn't do as he promised, but he ate two pieces of cake, and Kenzie did indeed watch.

After Erroll finished his cake, Kenzie proposed, "We can walk back to the train station now unless you can think of something better to do."

"No, I'm ready. We can sit on a bench there as well as here." During the walk back to the station, Erroll asked, "Are you ready to admit there's a Missouri? A sign over there says we're in it."

"All right, so there's a Missouri. We still don't know there's a place called Rounder, or that we have a farm there."

"I guess we'll have to wait and see, Kenzie."

They sat when they returned to Union Station. Their train to Rounder departed in the middle of the night, and arrived at Rounder on Wednesday afternoon, July 31, 1912. They walked from the train onto a simple outdoor platform at Rounder, instead of into another huge building like they found at previous stops. The train tickets Kenzie doubted, took them to a place close to their alleged farm, but they didn't know what to do next. They didn't know how to find the Mrs. Shier the salesman mentioned, and had never communicated with her, so she couldn't know they were in Rounder, even if she existed. The train left the station, and Kenzie offered a challenge. "We're about to find out if you talked us into a long trip for nothing, Erroll, and I think you did. I don't think there's a farm here. We're stuck out here in the middle of nowhere, hungry, tired, and with nothing."

He ignored her pessimism. "There's a man in the little building right beside us, Kenzie. Maybe he can tell us something; I'll ask him."

He stepped directly off the wood structure into the building. "We're here to see Mrs. Cecelia Shier. Do you know how we can find her?"

The guy in the building grinned, and replied, "Sure do. Cecelia lives here in town. She told me to watch for you and to ring her up when you come in. She's on the same line with the station, so I won't even have to go through central."

The man went to a device on a wall, turned a small crank two full turns, paused, did it again, then cranked it twice more, about a half turn each time. He talked at the center of the device, held a piece of it to his ear, and told Erroll, "Cecelia'll be here in about five minutes." As the man predicted, a lady in an almost new 1912 Chevrolet soon drove into a dusty lot by the wood platform. The man looked at Erroll, jerked his head toward the motorcar, and stated, "That's her."

Chapter 2
1912

Kenzie grabbed Erroll's arm, and pulled him over to talk to the lady. "Mrs. Shier? I know we smell bad and look a fright, but we're Kenzie and Erroll Paterson, and we think we bought your farm. Thank you for meeting us here."

Mrs. Shier looked the Patersons up and down. "Yes, I'm the person you want. I'm grateful you bought the farm. You're probably hungry and tired . . . Can I persuade you to come over to my house for supper before you go out to the . . . your . . . farm? I didn't expect you today, but have some whole fried chickens and cherry pie, and can cook more sweet corn in a hurry. Won't you come?"

Erroll broke into the conversation. "We really do appreciate the offer Mrs. Shier, but—"

Kenzie interrupted. "Mrs. Shier, we'd love to." She frowned at Erroll.

Mrs. Shier said, "Two things you need to know. First, don't call me Mrs. Shier; call me Cecelia. Second, I want you to succeed here, and before you succeed, you must eat right." Cecelia offered plenty of food to them, and though Erroll first tried to evade the invitation, he ate half the cherry pie.

Everyone finished eating, Cecelia and Kenzie washed the dishes, and Kenzie suggested, "Perhaps we should go out to see the farm if it's convenient for you now. We need to clean up, and we're about to die of curiosity . . . it'll be great if we get there early enough to look around before dark."

Mrs. Shier nodded. "Yes, I know you must be ready to end your journey. We're only about two miles away. Let's go outside and hop in my car; we'll head on out." Mrs. Shier cranked her car, drove south—less than a km past a one-room schoolhouse, about three km total—and turned off the dirt road into a driveway, near a tall and narrow house. "This is the house. Not fancy, but on a rock foundation."

Kenzie wiped tears from her eyes and replied, "Cecelia, it's a mansion. You can't imagine where we lived before we came here."

Mrs. Shier frowned. "I've seen my share of hard times too, Dear, and I hope none of us have to see those again. Do you want me to show you around?"

Erroll answered, "Yes, we'll appreciate it." Cecelia took them inside first. They entered the kitchen through the south door near the west end of the house, and saw a living room adjacent to the kitchen. Curtains graced the windows, a cook stove the kitchen, and a heating stove the living room. A steep, enclosed, twisting stair at the east end of the house led to two bedrooms upstairs, separated by a wall with a door opening covered only with a piece of cloth.

They went back downstairs and out the one door. The house faced a pump on a well outside the door, and a board barn about thirty meters downslope to the south. They could see a small pond dam about fifty meters upslope east of the house, a storm cellar occupied a place off the southeast corner of the home, and an outhouse stood about ten meters behind the cellar. Around back, they saw a couple cords of wood stacked against the house on the north.

Kenzie continued to dab mutely at her eyes. Erroll asked, "How much of the farm can we see from here?"

Cecelia answered, "There are eighty acres total, all in one plot, all east of the road. The farm extends both north and south from the house. A fence goes all the way around it, except for a hedge across the south end, and except for a detour around a ten acre hay field in the southeast corner, and another detour here around the house, cellar, and outhouse."

Erroll could see part of the fence, and the part he saw had five barbed wires with wood posts. He commented, "The fence looks tight and solid."

Kenzie pointed south. "Is the barn part of the farm?"

"Yes."

She next pointed east. "Whose cows are those?"

"They're mine, but I'll sell them to you if you want them."

"We don't have any money." Kenzie turned away from Cecelia.

"There are eleven cows. My nephew takes care of them now, but he'll be grateful if you take over the job. I'll sell them for $40 a head, and throw in the two small calves for free. If you want, I could add their price to the land price, to add $44 to your payment at the end of each year."

Kenzie asked, "Will we have to sign another contract?"

Cecelia looked directly at Kenzie, put her hand to her forehead, and questioned, "Another contract? I don't know anything about a contract."

Kenzie looked at Erroll and sniffed under her breath, "I told you."

Erroll reminded Cecilia, "Cecil Anderson had us sign a contract back in the UK. Perhaps we should have asked for a carbon copy, but we didn't. The contract said $400 a year for ten years, and we supposed you'd have that contract."

"I talked with Cecil on the telephone a couple of times, but never actually met him. I told him all I wanted was a handshake. The amount you specify is what we talked about, but I expressly told Cecil to ask only for a handshake. That's the way we do things around here. I once had a bad experience with a contract, and don't want another."

Erroll looked confused. "We did sign a contract. Can we still buy the farm?"

Cecelia shook her head and replied, "I didn't see a contract." After a moment, "Why don't we clear the air, forget the original contract, and shake on a new agreement that includes the farm at $400 a year, plus the cattle at $44, to get a total of $444 a year for ten years?" Cecelia shook hands, first with Kenzie, then with Erroll.

"Mrs. Shier . . . Cecelia . . . you're wonderful. You could have ruined everything for us, here and now, but you didn't. I didn't believe a place called Rounder even existed. How can we ever thank you?" Kenzie's tears flowed again.

Erroll put his arm around Kenzie, but Cecelia shrugged off her comment. "As I already said, that's the way we do things here. I trust you." She grinned. "You can't run off with eleven cows and eighty acres." She glanced toward the setting sun. "I'll soon go back to town and give you kids time to look around before dark, but first, I have a fried chicken and a peach pie in the car for you. I'll drop them off in the kitchen and go." She went to her car, removed the food, took it to the kitchen, came back to her car, cranked it, and went back up the road to the north.

Even before Cecelia's car disappeared from view, Kenzie put her hand on Erroll's arm and acknowledged, "You believed things would work out, and they did. I don't know how they could be better. I admit I wondered if there'd be any farm here at all, but this is more perfect than I could have imagined. It isn't at the McCarty level, but it's so much better than anything we could have dreamed about back home."

"Kenzie, this is our home. We live here now, and there's no longer a 'back home' in the UK."

"Yes, it's our home in a way, and it's magnificent, but it won't really be our home until we pay for it. We must think about that before we do anything or decide anything."

"Whatever, Kenzie, but we don't have to worry about payment today."

"We can't easily worry about anything as perfect as this house, but we must. We must worry about it today, and every second, until our new home is really and truly ours."

"Maybe. Let's look around." They walked through the rooms of the house—their house, according to Erroll—again. The house included furniture, but the beds upstairs had no blankets; they would later learn corn shucks made the rustling sounds they heard in the mattresses. Cecelia put food in the kitchen, but they found no other food in the house. They found a partial box of matches, a kerosene lamp about quarter-full of kerosene in the living room, and another about half-full in the kitchen. They looked in a pie safe in the kitchen, and discovered four plates, four cups, and four sets of fake-silver forks and knives. A Bible, a book on gardening, and another on carpentry, rested on a table in the living room. They noticed an empty metal bucket and an empty metal tub behind the cook stove, plus an empty teakettle on it. The storm cellar had bare shelves inside.

They came out of the cellar, and Kenzie commented, "Whew. It's hot here. Let's go back in the house—perhaps it'll be cooler there."

"Maybe. But do you want me to build a fire in the cook stove so you can heat water for a bath?"

"I suppose I do, but that'll make it even hotter in there."

"I'll do it, and'll pump water to mostly fill the teakettle and the tub. Maybe you can take the heat long enough for your bath."

Kenzie waited for water to boil in the teakettle, poured the hot water into the tub, and took a bath. Erroll checked out the pond and took his bath there. He came back to find Kenzie already dressed after her bath, but she complained, "Erroll, look at our clothes. They're filthy dirty, ragged, and torn, but we put them back on after our baths."

"What else can we do, Kenzie? We don't have more, do we?"

"That's my point, Erroll, we don't. I don't know how much

longer we can each get by with only one outfit." She wiped her brow. "You want some of the peach pie Cecelia left for us?"

They each ate one piece of the pie, then Erroll pumped more water, they removed their dirty outerwear again, and Kenzie washed the clothes in the tub, without soap. They went to bed before dark, and slept in their underwear on a bare mattress. Erroll thought the bare mattress a step up, because they slept on a rug on the floor in their former shack.

Chapter 3
1912

The Patersons awakened on their first morning in the farmhouse when the first glimmers of light came through the upstairs window. They went downstairs and planned their day as they breakfasted on part of the peach pie. Erroll stated his plan quickly. "I'll walk all over the farm today, look at the garden, look at the cattle, look at the fences, and see what's in the barn."

Kenzie protested, "Erroll, we need to make a list of stuff we absolutely must have soon, and decide how we can get it. On top of that, we need to talk about long-range goals."

"You make the list, Dear. I'll look at it when I get back and add anything I think of. As for a long range goal talk, we can surely push that back to a less busy time."

"You want to put off everything until later. I can go along with putting off the long-range goal talk, but we really need the first item on our short-range list. That item is to find something to eat today."

"We have fried chicken and a couple pieces of pie left, and don't forget the garden out back."

"Oh, I forgot about Cecelia's things. We'll have those, plus whatever I can find in the garden."

"All right, I'll go now, but will try to think of things while I look around." Erroll dashed out the door, bumped into a person standing outside, and nearly knocked his straw hat off.

"Watch out—I'm sorry. I didn't expect anybody to be here. Who are you?"

"I'm Ben Jones," The man used both hands to straighten his hat. "I came over to say hello."

"Oh. I'm Erroll Paterson. Come in and meet my wife."

"No, I'm afoot and need to go on back home."

"Where do you live?"

"Over yonder." Ben gestured vaguely to the north or east.

"I'm glad you came by. Come again when you can stay longer."

Ben didn't reply, but walked to the road and turned south.

Erroll watched a moment, then walked north beside the road, inside the line of the fence—he thought of the fence as his—walked around the edge of the garden a half hour or more, looked carefully at every plant, climbed over the house enclosure, and continued north until he came to the corner of the eighty. He turned east, followed the fence over a little ridge on the side of the hill, and then uphill more, all the way to the next corner, where he turned south. He saw the cattle under some shade trees over by the eastern boundary. The cattle ran in front of him, until they circled back to their shade trees. He noted their good condition, and saw the two little calves Cecelia mentioned the day before, both heifers.

He thought he saw a greenish-yellow hat through the corner of his eye, on the ridgetop east, but saw only grass when he looked again. He stopped to look at the ridge a moment, then continued south past a small spring, with water trickling down into a rock-lined pool with cattle tracks all around, and on south as far as the fence went. He followed the fence west and then south again, along the edges of the hay field Cecelia mentioned. It appeared the hay'd been cut, but could tolerate another cutting before winter. Erroll didn't slow, but continued to walk. He came to a drop off—a bluff—as he continued south. A dry creek bed cut across the southwest corner of the eighty along the bottom of the bluff, with a flat, tree-covered flood plain south of the creek. He came to the hedge Cecelia said formed the southern boundary of the eighty, walked west beside the hedge, crossed the creek, and walked farther west to the fence going north between the road and his land. He noted brush in the water gaps where the creek entered and exited his land, but supposed both would wash out when the creek flooded.

He walked north, back toward the barn and house he'd see after he climbed the bluff. He came to the barn and discovered a log hay feeder against the south side of it, under a high door. He went around the barn to the north side, and entered it through a regular-size door beside a wide sliding door. He looked around. The barn had a bin in the southwest corner, empty except for a few oat grains and some raccoon droppings. An empty enclosure north of the bin looked as if it once held chickens, with a roost, a waterer, a feed trough, and five nests. Two horse stalls on the north, east of the chicken enclosure, and two more directly opposite on the south, had no horses inside.

The wide door opened into a bigger area on the east side of the barn. The bigger area contained a buggy, a wheelbarrow, and a high-wheeled wagon filled with junk and hand tools. Several rough-sawn oak boards leaned against the back of the wagon. A groundhog burrow went down behind the wagon. A ladder went up against the north wall of the barn, between the regular-size and the wide door. Erroll climbed the ladder, went through a loft opening, and found a loft about half full of loose hay. A pitchfork stuck out of the hay to the left of the ladder, and the ladder continued up the north wall of the barn, to a hay door under the peak of the gable.

He came out of the barn and went to the house, where he found a man and woman talking to Kenzie. She introduced them as Ron and Jan Cline, their neighbors from directly across the road west. Jan wore a bonnet and long sleeved shirt; the bonnet covered a slightly pale face, and she acted friendly, but tough. Ron wore a straw hat over a suntanned face, had wide shoulders, a stature shorter than Jan's, and radiated a decisive personality, though he walked with a cane. Gray hair showed under the hat, and matched his gray eyes.

Jan asked questions about Scotland when Erroll entered the house, but Ron soon offered practical help, and began with a chicken deal.

"Banty chickens are about to pollute our farm. Is there any way you can take a dozen of 'em off our hands?"

Kenzie asked, "What's a banty chicken?"

Ron explained, "They're like any other chickens, but smaller. They lay eggs, and you can eat the eggs, except they're smaller, too. They sometimes sit on their eggs and hatch more banties. They did that at our place, and we have too many. You'll do us a great favor if you come over after dusk this evening, when we can catch 'em, and bring some back over here."

Kenzie enthused, "We didn't always like eggs in Scotland, but sometimes we had nothing else, and we relied on them for much of our nutrition. We'll be over this evening for sure—I can almost taste eggs already!" She paused. "Chickens won't stay here unless we pen them up a few days, so we'll have to find a—"

Erroll interjected, "There's already a place in the barn. But are you sure you want to give your banties away, Ron?" Ron grinned and said he'd like nothing better. Erroll responded, "We'll be over as soon as we think they're on the roost. We'll pull grass and weeds for them until we can let them out to find their own food."

Ron grinned again and continued to address Erroll, but on a different subject. "I want to tell you something about your cattle—do you know anything about cattle?"

"Yes, I spent my whole working life with cattle in Scotland."

"Great. Jim . . . Stone . . . Ed and Cecelia's nephew—borrowed my bull last winter. He only had 'im a couple months, timed for your cows to calve about now."

"They've started. I saw two young calves today."

"Then you should get the rest of 'em in a month, or two at the most."

"That's good to know. I noticed today there isn't a bull with the cows."

"Yeah. I don't know what you did in Scotland, but over here, we like to bunch the calves together, and to do that we keep the bull away from the cows most of the year. I have a strong bullpen, and only put the bull with my cows for a couple months to calve in the spring. Jim—and Ed Shier before him—borrowed my bull for late summer calves each year. The bull's a purebred Shorthorn, same as your cows. Because they're purebreds, people will come here and buy heifers and bulls from you—they'll get them, so you won't have to figure out how to take 'em to a market."

"I'll be grateful if I can continue that. What did Jim and Ed pay you?"

"They fed the bull. That's all the pay I need."

"Great. I'll remember that next fall."

Ron didn't reply quickly, so Jan began a different line of thought. "Ron and I . . . or just I . . . host a sewing bee at our house on Friday afternoons. That's tomorrow. I can't help but notice, Kenzie, the clothes you two wear look rougher'n a cob, and I wonder if you want to come?"

"Jan, I'd love to go, I really would, but I don't have sewing supplies. We left all that behind in the UK."

"That's all right. Several of the women don't have supplies. We have patterns, cloth, and everything anyone needs. We'll welcome you with open arms. I hope you can come."

"I'll be there, Jan. We didn't have neighbors in Scotland, and I didn't know what we missed."

Jan hugged Kenzie. "Wonderful. I'll look for you about two o'clock." Jan seemed to finish, but then added, "As for neighbors, some are better'n others."

Erroll switched back to another question about cattle. "Our loft's about half full of hay, Ron. Do you think that's enough for the winter?"

"I know exactly how much hay's there. I helped put it there, and it might be enough if we have a short and mild winter, but it'll be shy in a normal winter. Ed and I, then later Jim and I, traded hay work every year. Do you want to do that too?"

"I'm afraid I'm like Kenzie, Ron. I might want to, but I don't have horses, a mower, rake, or anything I need. I can't pull my weight. What happened to Jim?"

"Jim is Cecelia's brother's boy. He lives over in Jakesville, the Jake County seat. He works for the road department there, and it's real hard for him to regularly check on the cattle, put up the hay, and all the other stuff. I watched the cattle for him some, and fed them in bad weather. That's why Cecilia wanted to sell the farm. Jim's a good boy, but the farm seriously overworked him . . . all the same, I think Cecilia wanted to free me from the farm about as much as she did Jim. Don't worry about not having horses or equipment. Jim didn't have that stuff either, and Jan and I didn't when we moved across the road from the Shiers, but we helped each other. Jan and I are getting up in age now. We're pretty much at the top of our game, but that won't last. We're comforted to know you live across the road from us, because before you came, our nearest neighbors were the Millers up by the school, and the Joneses back behind your place. The Millers don't farm, and we're not keen on the Joneses."

Jan edged toward the door. "Come on, Ron. I have a fire in the cook stove. It don't take long to curry a pony, but I need to start supper before the fire dies."

Jan and Ron went across the road to their home, and Erroll talked about food to Kenzie. "We'll have milk and eggs right away. We'll go after banties this evening. I won't try to get the mamas of either of the new calves in the barn, but I'll load the next calf in the wheelbarrow and put it in a horse stall. The calf'll bring its mama to the barn often, and I'll take three or four pints . . . I suppose we can say a couple of quarts now that we're in the US—of milk every day. That way we'll have milk, eggs, and whatever you can get out of the garden, so we can forget about starving."

"Wonderful, Erroll. We're so rich we can adopt a baby next year. I checked the garden while you walked, and there are two long rows of potatoes there, plus other things. I dug a potato hill with my hands, and we can have new potatoes and peas, along with green beans, tomatoes, fried chicken, and pie for lunch today. When we can add milk and eggs, we'll be rich by anybody's definition."

Erroll grinned big, "Yeah. I saw all that stuff too. How soon'll you have that lunch ready?" After a pause, "What did you say about a baby?"

"I want a baby, and we can afford one, as soon as we have plenty of food."

"You're silly, Kenzie. You can't adopt a baby if I won't agree, and I won't."

"We can cross that bridge when we come to it."

"But not if I won't go across it with you. What did you say about us being rich?"

Kenzie grinned, and didn't answer the question. "I have to build a fire before I can cook anything." She sobered, and then went on. "It's so hot here I hate to build a fire, but it's better than cooking outside, like we did before we came here."

"Yeah, especially if it rains. Do you suppose it'll be as warm in winter here as it is hot in summer?"

"Maybe not, Erroll. Do you remember when Ron talked about hay in winter? He gave me the impression winters are even worse here than in Inverness."

"I'll ask about the winters here when I see somebody. Ron thought we should put more hay in the barn loft, and maybe next summer we will, but this coming winter, I think I'll herd the cattle in the hay field for a couple hours each winter day that I can. The herdsmen did that for McCarty's cattle, and saved a lot of hay. I'll make the fire for you, and then check on the cattle again after lunch. If Ron's right, we could have another calf any day now."

"Milk and eggs will be wonderful, but I'm not so sure about the sewing bee this afternoon. I'm torn. We can't afford to spend money until this farm is ours, even if it will be ours someday. I don't want to take free stuff from Jan, but we really do need the help."

"Yeah, I too abhor charity, and that's one reason I plan to herd cattle in the field instead of asking Ron to help us cut hay. But the sad fact is, Kenzie, we're poor, and we need all the help people offer us."

"Perhaps. We can start our days with clean clothes if I can make a second dress for me and a second shirt and pair of pants for you. Look over there." Kenzie pointed across the road. "Jan's clothes are drying outside in her yard—it looks like she suspended them from a wire. Can you put up something like that for me?"

"No, we don't have wire. Can you hang clothes to dry on a tree limb in the back yard?"

"Someday, if there's no other way, but I need to dry things inside until we get enough clothes I can be decent when I take wet things outside. We need clean clothes every day, and I hope to make more over at Jan's."

"I recently thought about something else, Kenzie. Thelma Bradley told us how to write to her, and wanted us to do it, to tell her if we got here safe."

"I already did it, Erroll; I borrowed a postcard from Cecelia. What's on your list for today?"

"I'll go down to the barn to figure a way to keep a calf there. Don't forget to call me when lunch's ready." He grinned.

"And don't forget to let me know when you're ready for the long range goal talk." Kenzie grinned back.

"Right." Erroll grimaced. "We might get around to that in a few decades, but now I need to get to the barn." Erroll found some rope and a couple wood gates in the barn he could use to close off one horse stall, and to make a narrow place in another, for a cow to stand while he milked.

He finished his work in the barn, and Kenzie called him to lunch. Kenzie continued to marvel at the new home. "I can't get over how great it is to have a house that will be ours, it's absolutely——"

"Right. Nobody can kick us out of it; not Unc., not anybody."

"Cecelia can, if we don't get our hands on 111 American dollars and hang on to them for a year." Kenzie stopped a moment, then suggested, "Maybe I should walk into Rounder and look for a job."

"I won't put up with that, Kenzie; we'll think of something else."

"Something like what, Erroll?"

"I don't know now, but we have a year. We don't need to worry about it today."

"We need to worry about it every second of every day, Erroll. Do you think we can keep a couple of heifers this year and increase our herd that way?"

"Maybe. Our income'll be down this year if we do, but up in later years. I'll ask Ron if he thinks we have enough grass for that. We don't have to decide that today either, regardless of what you might say."

Kenzie smiled. "Two extra can be a good thing if they up our income. But more in the here and now, the fire'll burn out in the cook stove this afternoon. I think I'll let it happen, and we can eat cold potatoes and tomatoes for supper, if that's all right with you."

"That'll be fine, Kenzie. I'll go check on the cows again, then think about how to make a barn lot." Erroll walked by the cows, and they acted normal and content. He saw Ben Jones up on the hill east of his pasture, near where he thought he saw a hat earlier. Ben wore the same greenish-yellow straw hat Erroll jostled that morning.

Erroll waved, Ben waved back, and approached the fence. "Hi. I'm Ben Jones. We met this morning; you can't see my house, but it's over the hill." He pointed. "My farm connects to the road in front of your place, with a long driveway that goes north from my house, then west past the schoolhouse."

"I'm glad to see you again, Ben."

"I'm a bundle of curiosity today. What did you pay Cecelia for your eighty?"

"We haven't paid anything yet, but will pay over ten years."

"How much will you pay?"

"Why do you ask?"

"No reason. I'm just curious."

"I don't know that it's a secret, but it might be better to ask Cecelia about that."

"Actually, I do have a reason to ask. I don't want to ask her, but I want to buy your eighty. I already have the eightys to your east and north, plus to your northeast. If I can buy yours, I'll have a half section in a block, and easier access to the road."

"I'll talk to my wife about it, Ben, but I don't presently think we want to sell. I don't know where we'll go if we leave here."

"You can stay right where you are. I'll hire you to look after the cattle and maintain the property."

"Again, I'll talk to my wife, but we recently left a situation like that, and we probably don't want to try again."

Ben's face smiled, but his eyes didn't. "Let me know if you change your mind." The smile left his face. "But don't trespass on my land."

"I haven't seen anything to make me want to trespass on your land, Ben. I'll tell my wife we talked." Ben turned, and walked up the hill, away from Erroll.

Chapter 4
1912

Erroll looked again at the cows, and he too turned and walked away, to his barn. He climbed to the loft and threw hay down to put in the nests in the chicken enclosure. When he finished with the nests, he picked up a one-man crosscut saw from the wagon, went down by the creek, and cut two good-size trees, before he thought the sun low enough in the west Kenzie might be ready with supper. He took a longer than normal way back to the barn, past the cattle by his eastern fence, and put the saw in the wagon. He pulled a shovel from the wagon and carried it in the house for Kenzie to use to dig potatoes. She wasn't ready with supper, but it took her only a few minutes to put out their two plates, two forks, a tomato, and two cold potatoes.

Kenzie commented about the house again after supper. "Erroll, how wonderful it is to live in this house. McCarty people would think it small and crude, but to me, it's perfect. I can't think of any tiny detail I want to change."

"Me either, Kenzie. But I talked with a guy named Ben Jones today, and need to tell you about it. He wants to buy this place. He can't have power over us the way Unc. did, but he somehow seemed a bit strange. I think we should be wary."

"Why?"

Erroll told Kenzie the details of his talk with Ben, and then went to the barn for two gunnysacks. He and Kenzie walked across the road and knocked on the Cline's open side door. Jan responded and invited them in, but Erroll declined. "We're not cleaned up. We came over to see if you think it's dark enough to catch banties."

"I'm sure it is. I last saw Ron behind the house; let's go see if he's still there." Jan came out the kitchen door and led the way around, where they found Ron in the garden. "Ron, the Patersons are here for the banties."

Ron carefully leaned his hoe against the side of the house, picked up his cane, and pointed with it. "That's the chicken house, over there to the west." The Patersons followed Ron into the chicken house, where he pulled eleven hens and a rooster—more than half his banties—off their roost, and put them in the gunnysacks Kenzie and Erroll held open. Erroll thanked Ron, then he and Kenzie took the banties to their new home in their own—at least for a time— barn. Erroll pumped a partial bucket of water from the well, and filled the banties' waterer.

He returned to the house, where Kenzie told him she found a sheet under one of the mattresses, and tore it in half. She said each of them could wear a half sheet, while she washed both their underwear and their outerwear. She laundered all their clothes, and they retired early, covered only by half sheets.

The crow of their banty rooster awakened them on Friday, their second morning on the farm. Kenzie told Erroll some of her thoughts. "Because you won't help me make long range plans, I did it on my own. Our first objective is to pay for the farm. I can wait until we pay for the farm to begin our second plan, and that's to adopt a baby. I'll go to the sewing bee at Jan's today as part of a short range plan. I want you to take the shovel to the garden—"

"Kenzie, I—"

"Don't interrupt me, Erroll. Use the shovel to dig a hill of new potatoes for breakfast, then build a fire in the cook stove, and carry in a bucket of water. I'll cook the two biggest potatoes. Look for eggs in the barn after breakfast. I'll have lunch ready at noon, and will take a bath soon after, before I go to Jan's. I don't know how long I'll be at Jan's, so supper might be a little late."

"About your long range plans—of course we must pay for the

farm, Kenzie. We don't need a special plan to know that. But adopt a baby? Do you know how old we'll be after ten years?"

"We'll be ten years older than we are now, Erroll, forty. Is that a problem for you?"

"You don't see adopting a baby at age forty as a problem?"

"No. Poppa took care of us all by himself. He gave us everything he had, nothing but himself. I'm grateful, and can't think of one additional thing he might have done for us, but it will be so much easier for us to raise one child together, than for Poppa to raise two, all alone. I can't stand the thought of us going through all our struggles, merely to die, be gone, and leave no one to carry on."

"To carry on what, Kenzie?"

"To carry on our memory, like we carry Poppa's memory. To enjoy the farm we plan to leave, to build on it, to achieve more than we will, and to raise our grandchildren. Our grandchildren will continue, and soar to heights we can't possibly imagine."

"Does the person to 'carry on' have to be an adopted child? Can't it be anybody in the next generation?"

"It can be, but who, Erroll?"

"I think you'll change your mind before you're forty. I don't agree with the idea of adopting a baby at all, but we don't need to argue about it today. I'll build the fire you want, then get the potatoes and go along with your plans for today." He did what he promised, and commented, "A potato'll really hit the spot this morning. We'll have eggs and milk soon, and they'll be a big bonus."

Before they ate breakfast, Kenzie asked, "What's on your list of things to do today?"

"I'll check on the cows first, and if they're all right, I'll cut more trees for a barn lot. I'll take an axe, sledge, and wedge down the bluff to trim and split this afternoon, and will carry some of the split rails up to the barn if I have time. And I'll check for calves and eggs again before lunch and supper."

They ate their boiled potato quickly and with gusto. Erroll went to look at the cattle immediately after breakfast, and found most, but not all, in their usual place. He looked for the missing two. He met one walking up the bluff, continued, and saw a new calf. The calf jumped up and ran after her mama so vigorously Erroll didn't try to catch her, but instead walked all the way down the bluff and across the dry creek, before he discovered the other cow among the trees south of the creek. She didn't have a new calf yet, but he thought one imminent. He ran and walked up the bluff to the barn, and came back with the wheelbarrow, plus rope. He arrived before the calf did, so he sat down to wait. A little bull calf slid out after about an hour. Erroll continued to wait until the calf stood and nursed, then he pushed the wheelbarrow to the cow, picked up the calf, set him in the wheelbarrow, tied the calf's front legs together and back legs together so he wouldn't jump out, and pulled the wheelbarrow backward up the bluff and into the barn. The cow followed, and licked the calf the entire trip. Erroll took the calf in the horse stall with a gate across it, untied the calf, removed him from the wheelbarrow, and let the cow in the stall. He did a futile check for eggs, and went to the house.

Kenzie met him at the door. "Did you find a calf?"

"Sure did. I put both cow and calf in the barn. We can't drink the milk for a few days, and in the meantime, mama and calf should be together. Can you change your plan so you already have your bath when I come in for lunch?"

"If you want me to. I'll do that before I put more wood in the stove."

"Good. I'll take the tub to the cow after lunch, and carry three or four buckets of water. We can leave the tub with the cow except when we want it in the house. I saw another calf this morning, too old for me to catch, but I should take another look at it. Then I'll cut a couple trees."

Erroll went out the door, over the ridge east to look at the ten cows and three calves, and came back to the barn for his saw. He went down the bluff and cut two trees, then went back by the barn to leave the saw; he admired the calf and discovered an egg before he left the barn. He took the egg in the house, and found Kenzie waiting with a sumptuous lunch. She ceremoniously put the egg in a place of honor inside a cup on a south windowsill before they ate.

Erroll might have taken a little nap after the meal, but Kenzie jumped to a sewing bee question. "Do you think I should begin with a dress for me, or pants for you?"

"Should it depend on the cloth you have? Whatever you decide will be fine with me."

"Won't it be wonderful when we can hang extra clothes in the west bedroom—clothes we don't have to wear every minute?"

"Yeah, I suppose it will." Erroll's tone betrayed his lack of interest.

Kenzie raised her voice. "I do the laundry around here, and I know for sure it will."

"You're right, Dear. Your life will be easier if we each have a change of clothes, but I'll be happy with those in whatever order you decide. Now, though, I'll start on my tree work. Should I work late, or do you expect to have supper ready before sundown?"

"Perhaps you can work a bit late, because I'm not sure when the sewing bee will end."

"That's fine with me. I'll trim and split this afternoon." Erroll left the house and walked by the cows again. He picked up his tools in the barn, went down the bluff, and worked all afternoon. He dragged the trimmed tree limbs across the creek and high enough on the bluff to be sure they'd never wash down the creek; they'd be available when he needed them to repair water gaps. He sawed the butt end of each tree into two twelve-foot sections—he continued to try to use American units of measure—then split each section into rails. He made fifty-seven rails from eight sections of log. The sun remained above

the horizon when he finished splitting, so he went up the ridge east
again. He didn't see anything unusual about the cows, he returned to
his rails, and carried them up the bluff to a location beside the barn,
two rails per trip. He made his last trip near sundown; almost a dozen
rails remained near the creek, but he saw Cecelia's motor coach in the
driveway, and he went in the house.

He found Kenzie, Jan, Cecelia, and a young woman there. Jan introduced the young woman as Mary Miller, wife of Emmanuel Miller;
Mary said she lived in the house across Ben Jones's driveway from the
schoolhouse. Kenzie giggled, waved a newspaper-wrapped package all
during the introduction, and when it ended, she challenged, "I bet you
can't guess what's in here."

Erroll looked at Cecelia and Jan. When they didn't offer a hint, he
admitted, "I have no idea. What's—"

Kenzie blurted, "Two changes of underwear for you and for me!"

"But we don't have any money. How'd you get that stuff?"

Jan responded, "Kenzie told us this afternoon, doin' laundry
with no spare clothes's like pushin' a rope uphill. Cecelia's next-door
neighbor owns a clothing store in Rounder. He's overstocked on some
items, and very much wants to be shed of those surplus things, so I
called Cecelia on the telephone, she came out in her motorcar, and
took us all to the store. Kenzie and Mary helped Henry, the store
owner, and we all came back here with underwear for Kenzie's family,
and for Mary's."

Erroll replied, "I can't fall for a tale about 'helping' somebody by
taking their stuff free. The clothes were free?"

Kenzie exclaimed, "Yes! Absolutely free!"

"We must pay for them when we can." Erroll frowned and shook
his head, but Cecelia actually stomped her foot.

"No! I won't stand for it. Henry . . . my neighbor . . . won't stand
for it either. He planned to give the clothes away, and you kids are
more deserving than anyone he knows—than I know—than anybody

knows. You keep the clothes, and if you ever try to pay for them, I'll know about it, and won't stand for it. Is that perfectly clear to you, Erroll Paterson?"

Erroll didn't answer, and the ladies dillydallied. They asked about the calves, about the garden, and about the eggs. Cecelia eventually went out to her motorcar, and came back with two dishes.

She explained, "I almost forgot. I have a couple extra fried chickens, so I brought one for you, and one for the Millers. Also, will you kids let me pick you up Sunday for church, then come to my house for dinner? I'll bring you back out here in the afternoon."

Kenzie answered this time. "We'd love that, but we don't have proper clothes," and Erroll reinforced her.

"We'd stick out like a couple of sore thumbs. Maybe in a year or so."

Cecelia commanded, "You kids be ready at 8:45 sharp. The Millers already agreed to go. Nobody wears fancy clothes at Rounder Church." Cecelia went out the door before they could respond.

Jan grinned. "You both need to take it easy and let people be your friends. That's all anybody wants to do. Cecelia always takes the Millers and us. You get yourselves ready by 8:45 on Sunday." Tears formed in Kenzie's eyes, bewilderment showed in Erroll's, and mirth in Jan's. Jan hugged Kenzie and repeated, "People want to be your friends; that's all anybody wants to do."

Kenzie composed herself, and brought up an old subject. "What are the winters like here?"

She directed her question to Jan, but Mary answered. "They're regular winters, cold, with snow and ice."

Erroll followed up. "How cold are they?"

He, too, asked Jan, and she answered. "I'm not sure what the average is, but we never have it anyway. The ground usually freezes the first time in November, then thaws and refreezes several times, before it stays froze through January and into February."

"Frozen ground doesn't sound good to me. The ground froze in the Highlands sometimes, but didn't stay frozen for long. Maybe it's colder here." Erroll frowned.

"You're dern tootin'. Ron and I don't have a thermometer, so we don't know how cold, but we do know the bottom drops out sometimes."

Erroll persisted. "Mary mentioned snow and ice. Do you have much of that?"

"Sometimes. December snow sometimes sticks until the middle of February or later. Other years, the ground's bare as a mangy houn' most of the winter. I suppose a aver'ge winter has snow on the ground about half the time from Christmas to late January. Ron usually starts to cut ice for cattle in December, and he cuts it nearly every day after that, until early March most winters."

"Wow. From what you say, winters surely must be be colder here, than in Scotland." Kenzie shivered.

"Yep, winter's uglier'n sin here. You better have plenty of warm clothes, hay, and food put back before winter hits."

"Thanks, Jan. We'll try to be ready for winter—and for church on Sunday." After a lengthy pause, "Does Cecelia's motorcar have room for her and for two couples, plus Kenzie and me?"

"No, she'll probably make two trips. It ain't a fur piece."

"She doesn't need to come out here twice. Kenzie and I can walk that far . . . what is it in miles?"

"Two miles, but Cecelia plans to take you."

"We might put up with that one time, but after we learn where the church is, we can walk."

"You can work that out with Cecelia. Right now I hafta run; Ron'll be in 'most any time, cryin' for supper."

Erroll turned to Mary and inquired, "Do you want Kenzie and me to walk with you to your house?" Mary tried to decline, but they walked with her. Erroll carried the dish with her fried chicken in it, and they finished the round trip in only about ten minutes. Kenzie reported during the return trip, "Jan had a great idea at the sewing bee today. You'll never guess what she thinks."

"I'm sure you're right, Dear, I'll never guess. Why don't you go ahead and tell me?"

"Jan thinks I can run a seamstress business. She offered to let me borrow needles, thread, and scissors, and I can have customers provide the cloth. She thinks I can earn up to two dollars a day. If I can do that for a few days over two hundred, I can make our farm and cattle payment next year."

Erroll frowned. "Jan's done a lot for us already. Do you really think you should borrow her stuff?"

Kenzie laughed. "Where's your vision for the future, Erroll? I'm supposed to be the doubter. I did all the sewing for Poppa and us for years, and I know I can do this. The only question is, how many customers will come out here, and I have to try it to know. In any case, I need to help with the farm payment, because the cattle alone won't do it."

Chapter 5
1912

"I'm dubious about a sewing business, but right now I have to carry rails across the creek and part way up the bluff. The sky looks like rain, and rails could float away if I leave them where they are. Can you hold supper long enough for me to move them?"

"I can hold it, because I don't have to do anything. Cecelia left us a fried chicken, remember?"

"Oh, yeah, and thanks, Kenzie. I won't even go in the house when we get back, but will go directly down the bluff. I won't need a lot of time, because I won't carry the rails all the way back to the barn, but will look at the cattle again, and take a bath in the pond again." He did all that, and went through the barn on his way to the house. The dusky sunlight didn't reach inside the barn, but he found and retrieved the tub from the horse stall, carried it outside, and dumped the water out of it. He took the tub to the pump and rinsed it well; then he took it inside for Kenzie to use for laundry. He pumped water into the bucket and emptied it into the tub several times. Kenzie lit one of the kerosene lamps before they sat down to eat a portion of their fried chicken.

Erroll chuckled. "This is our first night to be up past dark here."

Kenzie laughed too. "That's right. And we'll be up a little longer, because I want to wash your pants and shirt and my dress. I'm so glad to have clean underwear before I even start to wash."

"Yeah, I think we got a little more charity than we ought to take, but it's done, and it's great. How long you think it'll take to do the wash?"

Kenzie laughed again. "That depends on when you let me have your shirt and pants."

"You can have'em as soon as we eat, and you can have my old shorts too. Do you have a pair of new ones handy?" Erroll laughed again also.

"Yes, they're upstairs. Can you get the old ones off while I go get them?"

"Yeah, I'll have it all ready for you. Do you want a fire, or can you wash the clothes in cold water?"

"A fire'd be better, but I'm tired. Cold water'll be quicker, and I think I'll do it that way tonight."

They finished their meal, Erroll left his clothes in the kitchen, went upstairs to bed, and fell asleep before Kenzie joined him there.

They woke up Saturday, and could see it rained a small amount during the night, but not enough to change the dry look of their pasture. Erroll went back to his barn lot project. He carried the remaining rails up the top half of the bluff, marked out a lot thirty feet by twenty feet, cut four rails in half to use as posts and set those in the ground first. The post work took most of his Saturday, although he did make time to carry three eggs to the house and check the cows.

Jan came over Saturday morning, to bring Kenzie a bunch of corduroy, some buttons, and pieces of old blanket. She offered Kenzie her first paying seamstress job, to make four coats—one each for the Patersons and the Clines. Kenzie told Jan she wouldn't take money, but would accept the materials. Jan mentioned other help; she said Cecelia called her on the telephone, and promised to find business for Kenzie in Rounder. Kenzie commented about Cecelia's offer, to Erroll later, and acknowledged she didn't expect much. She cut out the corduroy outer coats along with the blanket linings, and finished the sewing and buttons that same day. She took the Cline's coats over before supper, and Jan said, "You're faster and better'n anybody in these parts. I expect you'll have about all the business in the Rounder area by a year from now."

"I hope to complete at least a few jobs by then."

"Don't worry. Cecelia'll see you have enough business to make you work your head off."

"I hope so. I must go back home, though, because Erroll came in the house before I left a few minutes ago. I plan to have hardboiled eggs tonight, courtesy of your banties, and they won't take long to prepare, but I need to go home and do it. I really do have to go back now."

"All right, Kenzie. Much obliged for the coats. They're the best we ever had."

Kenzie ran back across the road to discover Erroll already had a hot fire in the cook stove. She cooked two eggs and two potatoes. She told about her sewing work for the day, Erroll told about his barn lot work, and each professed to admire the other's achievement. Erroll brought the tub from the barn after they ate, and Kenzie washed all the dirty clothes.

They arose early Sunday morning, did their morning chores, and waited for Cecelia before 8:45. They'd never seen inside a church except for their wedding ceremony, but the Rounder Church people welcomed them, and Pastor Nick Thomas asked if they wanted to join the church. Erroll resisted. "We don't know much about any church, including this one. Maybe we should attend awhile before we decide."

Pastor Nick nodded. "You're probably right, and on top of that, I like to counsel people before they join. Do you want to set a counseling session for next week?"

Erroll held back again. "Next week doesn't give us much time. Can we wait a few months?"

"Sure," Pastor Nick invited them into his office to look at a calendar. "How about Tuesday evening, October 8, at 7:30?"

"Yeah, that should work; Kenzie and I don't do much after dark, and we can come."

Cecelia waited while Pastor Nick and the Patersons talked, and then invited them to her house for dinner, along with the Millers and

Clines. All accepted, and walked the roughly two blocks to Cecelia's house.

Cecelia served a massive dinner, followed by delayed dessert. She announced she planned ice cream, and asked the men to crank it; the other men showed Erroll how to do it. He and Kenzie didn't make up for a lifetime of ice cream deprivation, but they tried.

Pastor Nick had to leave for a meeting after dessert; everybody else stayed and talked most of the afternoon, and Erroll described his encounter with Ben Jones during the afternoon talk. Cecelia looked at the Millers, looked away, cleared her throat, and described an experience with Ben. "Ed and I had a contract with Ben to buy the eighty the Millers live on, and that's why I don't trust written contracts. We agreed to make payments for ten years, and we did for six. Somewhere along the way, Ben decided he didn't want to sell after all, and tried to buy it back, but Ed wouldn't sell to him. Ben got the land anyway, and I'll never forget how he did it."

Cecelia stopped, so Kenzie asked, "How'd he do it?"

Cecelia resumed. "He cut the fence between the two eightys, and toled some of our cows through the gap. When Ed discovered the cows, Ben threatened him with a rifle and told him not to trespass, but Ed went after the cows anyway—the land was ours, for cryin' out loud—and Ben sued him in court for trespassing, and got the eighty back. We paid each year for six long years, and lost every penny of our payments, along with the land. So be warned."

Erroll asked, "Can you give us advice?"

"You bet I can. Don't go after your cows if you ever see them on Ben's property, but ask Ron to use his telephone to call the sheriff in Jakesville. Don't make a move until he gets there."

Erroll turned to Emmanuel. "I don't understand everything. If Ben owns the farm north of us, why do you live there?"

"We rent the house from Ben. I work at the ice plant here in Rounder, and don't use the land at all, but I've never seen Ben use it either. I've never seen a cow or a sheep or a plow on any of it. He's aggressive about collecting rent from us, but aside from that, I don't have any complaints."

The group fell silent for a moment after the Ben Jones discussion, but then Cecelia asked Erroll, "How many calves do you have now?"

"We have four so far. Six cows look reasonably close, and I can't see evidence the eleventh will calve this year."

Cecelia nodded. "That sounds normal. Ed and Jim sometimes had a cow that didn't calve. There's a guy here in Rounder—Ron knows his name—he'll haul a cow to the stockyards in Kansas City if you have one that doesn't have a calf. Maybe you can save a couple heifers just in case."

"Yeah, Kenzie and I already plan that. Do you think the farm'll carry more than eleven cows?"

"Yes, most years. If you get a dry year, though, like this year might yet be, eleven is a load for it." Cecelia paused, and turned toward Kenzie. "I understand you did a great job on Ron and Jan's coats."

Kenzie smiled. "I hope so." She turned to Jan and asked, "Did you call Cecelia about the coats?"

Jan didn't answer, but Cecelia did. "Yes, Jan called me. Isn't she a jewel?"

"Jan and Ron are both great. I don't know how we could have better neighbors."

"Those two are the best, but watch out for Ben."

"I'll probably never see Ben, but I think Erroll's already on guard."

"Good. I have a couple customers for you. One's ready now, and I'll bring her out tomorrow afternoon."

Erroll didn't participate in the lady conversation further, but he, Ron, and Emmanuel talked, until Kenzie commented, "We should go on home so Erroll can look at the cows. You don't have to take us Cecelia, we can walk."

Cecelia bristled. "Nonsense. Why do you think I have a motorcar? I'll take you out there. Come on outside." She took the Patersons home and left a plate of ham, two dishes of beans, and two pieces of pie.

After Cecelia left, Kenzie asked, "You want to eat this food now, Erroll, or wait until supper?"

"I'm tempted, Kenzie, but I can wait if you can."

They waited, Erroll went to look at cows, and only found nine. He searched for the tenth, and found her nursing a new calf about halfway down the bluff. The new calf was their fifth. He went back to the house, where he and Kenzie ate part of the ham, and all the other food Cecelia left, and talked a few minutes before they went to bed.

Erroll asked Kenzie about items they needed to buy. "Do you have kerosene and flour on your list?"

"I don't have a list, Erroll, because I don't have money."

"We'll have it someday. Maybe it's a little frivolous, but if we had a twenty-two rifle, I could shoot us a squirrel or a rabbit for supper almost any time. The woods down by the creek are full of 'em."

"I don't know about a rifle, Erroll. We should get kerosene for the lamps before a rifle."

"You're probably right. And lard, and later, garden seeds."

"But we can't buy any of that, because we don't have money, Erroll, and even after we have it, we must save it for the farm payment. We don't want to lose our house."

"You're right, we don't have money now, but we should have some soon. If old calfless wonder out there doesn't come through, we'll sell her, and have a bunch of money."

"Or if I get some sewing customers. Do you think Cecelia will actually be out here tomorrow?"

"Yeah, I do. But I don't know how much you can make sewing."

"More than you'll make on cattle—oh, Erroll, I'm sorry I said that. I know the cattle increase in value every day, even though it isn't time to sell anything yet."

"Neither of us has brought in a cent yet, but maybe we will one of these days. Regardless, we ate well today, enjoyed good conversation, and today's been a good day. We can go to bed full and happy tonight, and I think it's time for us to do it." Kenzie agreed, and they retired early again Sunday night.

Erroll went back to his barn lot work on Monday, and also milked Suzy, as Kenzie called the cow in the barn. He milked a couple quarts, and allowed the calf to finish. He put Suzy out of the barn to find the other cows, knowing she'd be back in a few hours. Kenzie persuaded Erroll to help her dig all the potatoes in the garden; they estimated the yield at over two bushels, put the potatoes on shelves in the storm cellar, and praised God for them. They had potatoes for lunch, along with other garden produce, and milk.

Cecelia drove her motorcar into the yard with two passengers in it, soon after Kenzie washed the lunch dishes. Erroll went to the barn lot before Cecelia arrived, so Kenzie went out alone to greet the group, and to invite them inside. "Good afternoon, Cecelia." She turned to directly face the other two people. "Good afternoon, ladies. Please come in."

Cecelia introduced people after everyone entered the house. "Shirley and Tammy, please meet Kenzie Paterson who I told you about. Kenzie, this is Shirley Cottrell and her daughter Tammy. Shirley gave me the good news Tammy'll need a wedding dress in a few weeks, and I told her you're just the person to make it for her. Can you come with me to the car, Kenzie, to get the dress material?"

She went to the motorcar, where Cecelia advised her to charge $3 for the dress. Kenzie made marks on a string instead of using a tape measure, and asked Tammy to return Wednesday for a fitting. Tammy agreed to do it, and Cecelia said she'd drive her out. Cecelia asked, and received, permission to bring someone else out on Tuesday afternoon. Kenzie worked on the dress Monday afternoon, until Erroll finished the barn lot and came in for supper. She pinned the dress together and made it ready to fit by then, and she made an early supper of garden produce.

Kenzie's seamstress business boomed during the late summer of 1912, and she bragged about it. "Erroll, I made $28 in August, and $12 more during the first week in September."

Erroll wrote figures on a piece of paper. "You're on track to make most of our farm payment on your own, without cattle, but we need to buy sewing tools for you, and kerosene, too."

Kenzie counseled caution. "Maybe we ought to hold off on spending until we see how we do in winter."

"You can at least buy your sewing tools."

"I think we should hide the money instead, and keep it until we have enough for the payment; if we go over what we need, then maybe we can think about buying things."

"You're more cautious than you need to be, but I understand—up to a point. You know where we can hide the money?"

"Yes, it's already in an envelope hidden in the floor crack under our bed." Erroll accepted the information, but later had money of his own he wanted to spend. Ten of the cows had calves, the last on September 2, but the eleventh continued to look as if she wouldn't, so Erroll asked Ron about the cow hauler person Cecelia mentioned. Ron named the man as Rob Mercer, and offered to call him on the telephone. Rob arrived the next day with horses pulling a wagon with stock racks on it, backed the wagon to a barn door, and he and Erroll loaded the cow. Rob charged $4 for the two-day round trip, and explained he'd get a check in the mail, as would Erroll. The $39.68 check arrived a few days later, with the hauling charge already deducted.

Erroll found the check in the mailbox, and ran inside to show Kenzie. "Look what came in the mail today!"

She stopped sewing to look. "Good, Erroll. That almost doubles our savings."

"There's so much we need, and so urgently, I think we should buy some of it."

"What we need most of all, Erroll, is to make our farm payment next June 28. If we don't do that, nothing else matters."

"Oh, we'll do it. We can sell calves in May and they should bring in over half of it, plus you'll bring in over half of it too. What do you need most?"

"I need $444, Erroll. When we have that, we can talk about buying things."

Chapter 6
1912

"I think we need at least five gallons of kerosene, and a couple gallons of lard for the house. I could bring meat to the table almost every day if I had a twenty-two rifle, and I could raise more garden stuff than you can imagine, if I had money to buy seeds."

"We won't need garden seeds before spring, Erroll, and I think Ron has a rifle you can borrow. But maybe you're right about lard and kerosene."

"I hate to borrow from Ron or from anybody, but if I do I should at least have my own shells, and those'll take money. I'll need to walk to Rounder to cash the check at Rounder Bank. How will it be if we both go, you take ten dollars to spend, I take ten dollars to spend, and we put almost twenty dollars in the envelope?"

"We can stay home and put almost forty dollars in the envelope, Erroll."

"Yes, but there's so much we really need."

"Perhaps. I don't want us to waste even one cent, but we do need some things, and maybe ten dollars apiece won't kill us. I'll agree to whatever you think, up to ten dollars."

"Great. How about if we go now?"

"Now? I have too much to do now. Why don't you go now, and just cash the check? Then we can go and buy things later. I'll work on lunch while you're gone. I plan scrambled eggs and tomatoes, and will have the fire and the tomatoes ready before you're back."

Erroll walked to the bank in Rounder, cashed the check, and returned. During lunch, he anticipated his purchases. "I think I can afford kerosene—we'll need that when the days are shorter—two hundred pounds of chicken feed—the banties'll need feed on snowy days—and new shoes for you and for me. We'll need new ones before winter."

"Erroll, you can't carry two hundred pounds of feed."

"You're right. I'll have to buy it fifty pounds at a time, but the banties won't care if we bring it all at once, or spread it out."

Kenzie laughed. "We do need all that. And I need laundry, sewing, and cooking supplies. Eggs'll taste better if we buy lard, and we can have gravy if I buy flour. I can go tomorrow before lunch if that works for you."

"Great. How about we leave at 8:30?"

"I'll be ready."

They walked to Rounder the next day, and bought everything on both lists except chicken feed, plus sugar, salt, pepper, and matches, and stayed inside their budgets. Kenzie came home with over two dollars, and Erroll almost one, after he subtracted the amount the chicken feed would cost.

They attended Rounder Church every Sunday, usually with transportation and dinner provided by Cecelia; Pastor Nick reminded them each Sunday of their October 8 counseling appointment. They talked at dinner the Tuesday of the appointment. "Do you remember what time we agreed to meet Pastor Nick, Erroll?"

"Yes, he reminded me Sunday, but I already remembered. We meet at 7:30, so we need to leave here five or six minutes before seven."

"I think he'll ask us to join Rounder Church, Erroll, and I want to. Do you?"

"Of course. What else do you think might come up?"

"I have no idea, Erroll. As you often say, I suppose we have to wait and see."

They showed up a couple minutes early at the church, but Pastor Nick invited them into his office as soon as they arrived. He asked them to sit, and then asked, "What do you know about Christianity?"

Erroll could think of nothing, initially, so the more talkative Kenzie answered. "Poppa—that's really Erroll's dad, but he raised us both—read to us from the Bible every Sunday. Since Poppa died, Erroll reads to me every day. We know what the Bible says about Israel's history, and about Jesus."

Pastor Nick smiled and responded, "Purely out of curiosity I'll ask you a lot more about your Poppa, Kenzie, and why he raised you instead of your parents, but first, what do you know about Jesus?"

"We know a lot, but Erroll really should answer that question."

Pastor Nick turned in his chair. "Erroll?"

"The most important thing we know about Jesus is the sacrifice He made for us. The effect of that hit me hard one day in Scotland, when I read the book of Romans to Kenzie—the part in chapter seven where the writer said he didn't understand why he did bad, and generally admitted he wasn't perfect, just as I know I'm not. But in one of the earlier Romans chapters, he wrote that because of Jesus' sacrifice for us, He could make us the same as perfect to God—as if we never did anything wrong. It took us a while to comprehend that, and to accept it, but now that we have, we know however we mess up, Jesus is right there with us, to point us right and to forgive us. We think that's the biggest thing, but the Bible also has a lot of detail about Jesus' birth and boyhood. Is that the part you want to know?"

"I think you're an eloquent speaker, eminently qualified to be a member of Rounder Church. Are you ready to join our congregation?"

Erroll repeated his earlier words to Kenzie. "Of course."

Pastor Nick then asked about Kenzie's Poppa, and she and Erroll described their entire family history, including the part they knew only from John's story about how Darlene and Ralph abandoned Kenzie. Pastor Nick offered them coffee, but they begged off and walked back home. They joined Rounder Church the following Sunday, on October 13.

Kenzie continued to attend Jan's Friday sewing bees. She made two dresses, and two shirts and two pairs of pants for Erroll. Jan suggested she cut the legs out of Erroll's old pants, and use them to line the legs on one of the new pairs, so she did, and also made a pair of lined pants for Ron, and finished them all before November.

Erroll wasn't busy after the calves came, so he used the shovel to 'spade' most of the fenced and grassy area around the house, to prepare for an expanded garden in 1913. He also had time to read the gardening and carpentry books that came with the house.

He continued to check on the cows after they calved, but only once a day, and never found a problem until a week before Thanksgiving. The day began cold and blustery, so he looked first in the woods below the bluff, but didn't find all his cows there. He walked north, past the hayfield, and noticed three cows and three calves east of his fence. He walked closer, and saw Ben Jones standing by the fence. The fence was cut, and the escaped cows licked corn off the ground.

Ben and Erroll faced each other without talking, for a good two minutes, each on his own side of the fence. Then Erroll quietly instructed, "Drive'em back over here, Ben, and I'll fix the fence."

Ben abruptly turned around and walked over the hill east. Erroll watched Ben until he couldn't see him. He pivoted also, walked toward his house, past it to the Cline house, and knocked on the door.

Jan answered the door and Erroll talked immediately to her. "Do you remember what Cecelia told me about the problem between Ed Shier and Ben Jones?"

"Shoot, yes. I remember what she told you and I remember the problem directly. Ron and I lived across the road from them, here in this house, when it happened."

"Do you remember that Cecelia advised me to call the sheriff if it happened to me?"

"Yes, I remember. Did—?"

"Yes, Ben cut my fence today, and he has some of my cattle. Will you use your telephone to call the sheriff?"

"No, get your fanny in here and use it yourself. The telephone's here in the kitchen—step in here and do it."

"I'd a lot rather you do it, Jan. I never used a telephone, and don't know how. Will you do it?"

"I suppose so. What will you do while you wait for the sheriff?"

"Nothing. I'll go on home now, but don't forget to call."

"No chance. I'll get'er done before you cross the road."

Chapter 7.
1912

Jan called the sheriff on Thursday, November 21, but he didn't show up in his motorcar until Friday afternoon. Erroll believed the remainder of his cattle went through the cut fence and over the hill east early on the first day, because he couldn't find them in his own pasture. The sheriff arrived and introduced himself as Steve McCoy, sheriff of Jake County. He was short, slim, and unarmed. He asked Erroll to explain, and he did. The sheriff inquired curtly, "What do you need me for?" He added, "Go after 'em," and turned to walk to his car.

Erroll ran to a position in front of the sheriff. "Wait. I can't. Do you know what happened to Ed Shier a few years ago?"

"I never heard of Ed Shier. What happened to him?"

Erroll recounted the story Cecelia told, but the sheriff remained unconvinced. "Can anybody around here back that up?"

"Yes, Ron and Jan Cline, straight across the road from here."

The sheriff didn't speak to Erroll further, but crossed to the Cline house and knocked. Jan came to the door, the sheriff identified himself, and Jan called Ron to the door. "Oh, hello, Ron. Your neighbor told me some nonsense about why he can't round up his cattle after they got out. He says you can back up his story."

"You bet I can back it up, and you can look up court records to show Ed Shier lost eighty acres to Ben Jones in exactly the same kind of scheme. You need to take it seriously, Steve."

"What's your name, Son?"

"Erroll Paterson."

"Erroll here told me he's afraid to walk on his neighbor's farm to go after his own cattle."

"He'll commit legal suicide if he does that, sheriff. My wife, Jan, called you, and we hope you can tell us something legal, so Erroll can get his cows back."

"He can round up his own cows."

"Ben warned Erroll not to trespass, the same as he did Ed. Ed's cows didn't get out accidentally—Ben cut the fence. And when he went for his cattle—he went onto his own land, by the way—Ben accused him of trespassing, and somehow ended up with eighty acres of Ed's land."

"I'll check into it, Ron, but don't expect me to discover anything. Where can I find Ed Shier?"

"Ed's dead, but his widow lives in Rounder. I don't know her address, but to get there, go on this road," Ron pointed, "into Rounder. Her house is third on the west after you pass the city limits sign."

"This is the wildest tale I've heard lately, but I'll talk to her." Just before he walked back across the road to his car, he added to Erroll, "I'll stop back by your place on my way to Jakesville, after I talk to the widder."

The sheriff crossed the road alone, because Erroll stayed to talk a moment with Ron. "The sheriff wasn't as interested in my cattle as I hoped he'd be."

"No, but if he keeps at it, he'll discover what you're up against. I don't know the legal way to handle it, but he can figure it out if he tries."

"I need to go home and tell Kenzie."

Kenzie already knew about the problem, but didn't know what happened with the sheriff, so Erroll told her, and told her his worry. "We don't have any cattle left, except for the calf in the barn, and I'll have to feed him chicken feed, I guess. He has to eat something. I can fix the fence, but if I do, the cows can't get back home. Ben may have figured a way to steal them from us."

"Better the cattle than the farm, Erroll."

"Yes, but best if he gets nothing. I hope the sheriff finds Cecelia at home, and she can get more across to him than Ron or I did. The farm's not much good without cattle on it, even if we don't lose it."

The sheriff delayed his return longer than Erroll expected, and wore a sober face when he showed up. "Mrs. Shier told me about Ben's methods, and she told me where he lives; I went to see him before I came here, and saw a bunch of cattle in a corral by his house. I don't know if they're yours, but Ben's home, and I asked him. He says they're his. I told him he's all right if they truly are his, but I'm on the way back to Jakesville to get a search warrant, and if they're not his, he'd best put them back on your place and fix the fence before I get here on Monday with that warrant. He laughed at me, and I don't expect much."

Erroll went over the ridge to look at the fence that afternoon, and a couple times on Saturday, but the gap in the fence remained, and he didn't see his cattle. He put chicken feed on the ground for the calf in the barn, but the calf didn't eat any of it as of Saturday. Cecelia came out to take Kenzie and Erroll to church on Sunday. They went to Cecelia's for dinner afterward, but didn't enjoy the meal as much as they might have, because of the missing cows. Cecelia warned Erroll he must not take matters into his own hands, and expressed confidence in the sheriff. She said, "I told the sheriff everything I knew, before he left here on Friday. I don't know if he thinks I lied, but I have a reputation as a straight shooter; if he doesn't believe me, all he needs to do is ask around. Sheriff McCoy's your only hope, Erroll. Ben'll have your whole farm if you give him any opening at all, and then you'll be homeless, and I'll be out payment for it, so don't play Ben's game. The sheriff can handle it, and if he doesn't get on it, I'll pester him until he does."

Jan added, "Ben's like a bull with one horn. He can destroy stuff, but his head's not all there, if you know what I mean."

The Patersons visited with people at Cecelia's after lunch until about three o'clock, and then lost their usual argument about walking home. Cecelia took them, but remarked about the threatening sky. "Maybe it's good you're almost home. I don't want to try this car on snow, and you don't want to walk in it, but it looks like we could have some this afternoon."

Kenzie nodded, but didn't say anything. Erroll noticed Suzy at the barn door when Cecelia turned into their driveway, waited until Cecelia backed out of the driveway, and then pointed and yelled, "Look! There's Suzy! Her calf'll be glad to see her. I'll go down and let her in the barn before I come in the house. Maybe I should also go over the ridge and look for the other cows."

Erroll put Suzy in the barn with her calf, went to the top of the ridge, and saw the fence wires back in a straight line, but didn't see cows. He turned south, and found them hiding from the wind below the bluff. He stood still, admired them for a couple minutes, and counted them. Then he walked back along his east fence to check the patch job, called it first-rate, and returned to the house to tell Kenzie. "It looks like the sheriff won't need a search warrant after all. The cows are all in our pasture where they belong, and the fence is fixed. You think I should have Jan call the sheriff on her telephone before he comes back out here?"

"Magnificent, Erroll. I admit I didn't expect Ben to do the right thing—maybe after he took the cows, it was already too late to do the right thing—but as you said Friday, we need those cows. Better late than never."

"Do you think I should go see Jan?"

"Oh. Yes, I think you should; what do you think?"

"Yeah, I think so too. The sheriff's probably not in his office now, but I can tell Jan now, and she can ring him up whenever she wants. I think she and Ron wanted our cows back as much as we did, so they'll be happy they're back."

Erroll went back outside for a few minutes and returned. "That's done. I still need to water the chickens, look for eggs, and let Suzy back out, but it might be early for that."

"Sit down and rest an hour. You worried yourself sick about those cows, and I'm glad they're off your mind—I'm going to kiss you until you beg for mercy."

Erroll laughed. "Lots of luck with that. I'll cooperate, but you can't make me beg." Kenzie made an energetic and prolonged effort, but Erroll not only didn't beg, he switched from defense to offense. He didn't make her beg, either.

Kissing exhaustion set in after many minutes, and Kenzie marveled, "Erroll, I can't believe how much our material well-being improved in less than a year. Do you realize we lived in a one-room shack, you worked for our awful Uncle Eric, and we had to fear Dumb Dal as recently as a year ago? And it got worse from there, and didn't improve until a mere four months ago?"

"Yep, Kenzie, we have it made now." Erroll's grin gave way to a long laugh.

"We're about to go into winter with a better chance of survival than I can remember, Erroll, but still, I wish you wouldn't say we have it made. Something bad always follows when you say that."

Erroll laughed again. "You think I can put a hex on us?"

"Let's just say I'll be afraid to go outside tomorrow."

"You're full of crazy talk, Kenzie. I think I'll go out and take care of the animals before snow flies." Erroll went out, and came back fifteen minutes later with three eggs. Kenzie didn't prepare supper, because she served stewed apples and cake Cecelia left. They retired early that evening, and heard the wind blow during the night, but felt surprise when they looked out the next morning at deep and drifted snow.

Erroll recalled a Kenzie statement. "You said last night you'd be afraid to go out today. Maybe I can see why." They laughed. Erroll didn't go out before breakfast as he sometimes did, but afterward he checked on the cattle, made sure they could find water at the spring, let Suzy in the barn again, and milked his daily two quarts before he allowed the calf to finish. He went to the loft, and threw hay down into the feeder below, for the first time that winter. Then he crossed the road to see if Ron needed help. Jan said Ron went out early and she thought he might soon finish with his chores.

Erroll went back inside with Kenzie, added wood to the fires in both stoves, and commented, "We have plenty of wood for this winter, but I'll have to cut some for next winter."

Kenzie fretted about her business. "Cecelia planned to bring a new customer today, but I bet she won't do it now, because of the snow. The mailman should have been here by now, but he's not. I don't know if he'll be absent, or only late today. And if the sheriff meant to come today, he probably wouldn't have."

"Yep, it's a good day to stay close to the fire. Isn't it great we have a warm house with two stoves? That's something you can add to your list of things we didn't have a year ago."

"True. That list could go on and—I think I hear the mailman. You want to go out and see if he brought mail?"

"Yeah, I'll go." He went out, and returned. "We didn't get anything except a notice about registered mail, or something, at the post office. The notice is addressed to you. You know what it could be about?"

Chaper 8
1912

"I know nothing about registered mail Erroll, but it isn't worth walking into Rounder on a day like this, whatever it is."

They talked more, until shortly after lunch they heard a knock on the door, and opened it to see Ron. "My horses are hitched to a wagon to go to Rounder. I could put the trip off a day, but somebody needs to bust the drifts. You want to go along?"

"I don't really need to go—well, Kenzie has something at the post office. I could go and see what that's about."

"I left the wagon out on the road. Come on." Erroll had to hustle to keep up, and put on his coat and hat as he went. Ron stopped at the post office first and Erroll jumped off the wagon. He asked for Kenzie's mail, received it in a regular size envelope, put it inside his coat in a shirt pocket, and waited outside in front of the post office for Ron to come back. Ron returned, took him back home, and Erroll carried the envelope in the house.

Kenzie asked, "What is it?"

"I don't know. It's addressed to you and I didn't open it."

"Go ahead and open it. If it matters to me it matters to you too."

Erroll opened the envelope, took a quick look, then gasped. "You better look at this too, Kenzie."

"I'm really kind of tied up. Can you read it to me?"

"If you want. It's from a retirement home in Rochester, New York, about someone described as an 'indigent woman,' named Darlene Dyer Cox Wilhelm Rodriguez. Do you suppose she can be your mother?"

"Wow! I don't know. Let me see that." Kenzie took the letter, and then read part of it to Erroll. "Dear Mrs. Paterson:" Kenzie stopped, and her eyes scanned downward before she read again, from the top.

"We're looking for Mrs. Rodriguez's relatives. We have a contact in Missouri named Nick Thomas, and he thinks you are a possible. If you are, please acknowledge to

> Good Times Retirement
> 4742 Canalfront Drive
> Rochester, New York"

Kenzie had been standing, but she suddenly sat. "Do you think it's possible?"

"Poppa talked about a Darlene Cox. I don't know about any of those other names. Does the letter say how old she is?"

Kenzie looked again at the letter. "No, it doesn't. I dreamed all my life about finding my mother, but it's a better dream than reality. The letter's signed by a Barbara Welborn. She doesn't say what she wants from us, but because she uses the word 'indigent', she might want money. We don't have money to send and we don't have it to pay for a trip there to talk to her. What do you think we should do?"

"We have to answer that letter, Kenzie. I don't know what we'll say in an answer, but we have to say something."

"Do you think we can act like we never saw the letter, and they'll let it drop?"

"No, and we can't do that."

"Erroll, we're about to get on our financial feet, and if this person is my mother, she'll knock us back off. I think we should say we never heard of her, and that's probably true."

"I don't agree, Kenzie. Let's at least pray about it, then talk to Pastor Nick about it on Sunday, before we put her out as trash."

"Poppa told us Darlene ran out on me."

"Do you remember back in Scotland when you jumped all over me for saying we can't be picky about right and wrong? And you insisted we not only can be picky, we must?"

"Yes, I remember."

"This is like that time. Maybe Darlene ditched you, but that doesn't make it right for us to ditch her. I still say we should pray about it, and I can't imagine God will tell us to do anything that looks like a dump."

"I'll pray about it too, but if God loves us, I know he'll tell us not to blow our money on indigent people. That woman doesn't deserve anything from us whatsoever, whether she's my mother or not."

"I don't know if you're wrong or right Kenzie, but what she deserves doesn't matter. Does God make us deserve his love? Do Ron and Jan and Cecelia make us deserve their help? Anything we can deserve is fine, but we have as much reason as anybody to realize undeserving people need help too. I don't know what we should do, and I won't try to convince you of anything, but we do need to pray— both of us do."

They prayed often, all week long. Cecelia didn't come after them in her motorcar on Sunday because of the snow, so they walked to church. They arrived early and asked Pastor Nick if they could talk with him after the service. He agreed, and when the time came, Kenzie described the letter they received, and asked his opinion. Pastor Nick asked, "Do you think the person is your mother, Kenzie?"

"We're not sure. The little we know is consistent with her being my mother, but what we don't know is more than what we do know."

"I must tell you I went to seminary in New York, and New York retirement homes write to me occasionally about various issues. A recent letter pertained to your mom—or this lady, whoever she is. I gave them your name and address as someone who could possibly answer their questions. Does the letter say what they want?"

"Only that they want us to acknowledge something—maybe that we received the letter?"

"They probably want you to acknowledge the lady could be your mother. What do you think are the chances?"

Kenzie grudgingly admitted, "It's possible, but I can't put a number on it."

"Of course. What do you think you should do?"

"That's the rub. Erroll thinks we should write a positive answer, and I think we should forget it. We wouldn't have brought this up to you, except Erroll insisted."

Pastor Nick smiled, and then shook his head. "Well, I can't tell you what to do, except to recommend you pray about it."

"We did that. Erroll insisted on that too. How long should we pray?"

"How long have you prayed?"

"A week."

"If you don't have a clear answer yet, maybe it's time to be still in the Lord's presence, to stop asking and merely wait for an answer."

"We came here to ask what you think."

"I can't tell you, Kenzie. I'm an outsider and won't bear the consequences of your decision. That's something for you and Erroll to decide."

"Well, thank you, Pastor. Are you going over to Cecelia's today?"

"No, she invited me, but I can't go today."

"We'll see you next Sunday then." Kenzie stood, then Erroll did, and they offered their hands to Pastor Nick, who shook them both.

After dinner at Cecelia's, Kenzie mentioned the letter to the entire group. The men didn't respond, but Jan, Cecelia, and Mary congratulated Kenzie, seemed to anticipate she would pursue a possible relationship, and that the lady would indeed turn out to be her mother. They walked home that day, and Kenzie talked as she walked. "That stupid woman can derail our farm payment goal just when it looks like we might reach it. We can't let that happen, Erroll."

"Maybe paying for the farm shouldn't be the most important goal."

"What could be more important?"

"Did Poppa put us first, or money first?"

"We were all Poppa had. He didn't have anything he needed to pay for."

"But would that have been true if he hadn't put us first?"

"I don't know. Maybe it wouldn't have. Maybe you're right. I don't really think you are, but if you'll write a letter for me to sign, I'll sign it. I have two stamps left, and we can put it in the mailbox on Monday."

"Kenzie, I can't write your thoughts. I'll write if you tell me what to say, but I can't make up anything for you."

"All right. Say she might be my mother, and ask what they want us to do if she is."

"Great. I'll write that as soon as we get home, even before I let Suzy in the barn."Erroll wrote the letter, Kenzie signed it, and Erroll put it in the mailbox on Monday. They had to explain they didn't yet have an answer when they met their friends at Cecelia's the following Sunday, and everybody accepted that, but grumbled about the nursing home, even though they didn't claim to be responsible for Darlene.

A reply came on Monday. Erroll checked for mail, found the letter, brought it inside, and gave it to Kenzie. "I'm afraid to open it, Erroll."

"I can understand that Kenzie, but I know you. You're going to open it, and soon."

Kenzie did indeed open the letter, which asked her to either send $40 each month to pay Mrs. Rodriguez's keep, or to come to the retirement home, pick her up, and take her to her own home. Kenzie read the letter aloud, frowned, and reprised earlier thoughts. "We can't do either of those, Erroll. We can't come up with the money, and we can't go to New York. So where does that leave us?"

"I wonder if the retirement home can send her to Rounder at their expense?"

"What if they do, and the lady turns out not to be my mother?"

"Maybe they need to ask her some things so you can know before she comes."

"That would work, Erroll, presuming they'll pay for her trip here, but I know they won't."

"You wanta try it? You'll be stuck with another letter exchange, but you can write a letter to tell them you want more information before you decide." Kenzie agreed, wrote the letter, and received a reply on Monday again.

A letter from the retirement home arrived, and said Mrs. Rodriguez didn't know her name and couldn't answer questions. Someone would travel with her, and they would arrive at the Rounder train station on Thursday afternoon at 2:30, only three days away. Kenzie fumed. "When did we say we think she's my mom? When did we say it's all right to show up like that? What if we decide to send her back?"

"They do seem overly hasty, don't they? If the lady doesn't know her name, I don't know how we'll know, or anybody'll know. Maybe she's not as bad as they say. We'll have to wait and see."

"Can we do anything besides wait, Erroll?"

"I think there's only one thing we can do, and that's meet the train on Thursday. She probably can't walk home with us if she's senile, but I bet Cecelia will haul her out there if the road isn't too muddy."

"You want to take her home with us, just like that? Have you thought about where she'll sleep, what she'll cost us?"

"I suppose she can sleep in our west bedroom. As for cost, we don't pay much for ourselves to live, and she'll have to live like we do."

"None of that will work Erroll. If she sleeps in the west bedroom she'll walk though our bedroom every day. And what if she likes steak or something we don't have?"

"Won't she be better off with us than out on the street in Rochester?"

"Erroll, you know they won't put her out on the street."

"The question is, will you put her out on the street?"

"That's unfair, Erroll. You know I won't."

"Then we have to meet that train, don't we?"

"Perhaps we do. I'll ask Cecelia if she'll go with us." Cecelia and the Patersons met the train on Thursday, December 19, 1912.

Chapter 9
1912 – 1915

The train arrived on time, and Mrs. Rodriguez's traveling companion helped her off, whereupon Erroll pointed and yelled, "That's you, Kenzie! That lady has to be your mom! She can't look like that and be anybody else!"

"I suppose you're right, Erroll. I think we're stuck, but she looks like she doesn't know anything. Let's talk to the other woman and learn what we can."

Kenzie introduced herself to the second woman and continued, "I think she's my mom, but I was separated from her when I was about a year old. Why does she have so many names?"

"She came to us with a stack of papers. Her birth certificate shows she was born in Rochester in 1856 as Darlene Dyer. Then she married a Ralph Cox in Rochester, Oscar Wilhelm in San Francisco, and Tony Rodriguez in Rochester. Our administrator independently learned Mr. Rodriguez died in 1911, the day before Darlene, as we call her, came to Good Times. An anonymous neighbor dropped her off. She couldn't care for herself, had no known income or net worth, and we never received a dime for her keep. I'm so glad we found you, because I know she'll be in good hands with you. I'm going on to Kansas City, so I need to re-board the train now."

Cecelia smiled big. "Kenzie, you must be so happy to find your mother after all these years. I wish she could know you."

Erroll took Darlene's arm and helped her to Cecelia's car; he and Kenzie lifted her into it. Cecelia drove them out to the farm, where they helped Darlene out of the car, into the house, and into a chair. The confused look obvious on Darlene's face when she struggled off the train, remained throughout the trip to her new home. Cecelia hugged Darlene, then Kenzie, and assured her, "I know you'll be so happy now." Cecelia let herself out and drove back toward Round-er.

Kenzie exhaled, looked at Erroll, and wondered, "Can we get her up and down the stairs every day?"

"I don't think we can, Kenzie. Can we make a place for her to sleep down here?"

"I suppose we can bring a bed down for her, but it'll take up a lot of space."

"We'll hafta take the bed apart, because it won't come downstairs in one piece. I'll do that." Erroll brought the pieces down the stairs, and then prepared to reassemble the bed in the living room. "Where should we put it, Kenzie?"

"How about behind the stove?"

"I don't think it'll fit there, and if it does, it'll be hot."

"Where else can it go?"

"The only place I can see is at the foot of the stairs. We might have to squeeze around it when we go upstairs, but I think that's the best place."

Kenzie shrugged. "Put it anyplace; I can live with it."

Kenzie and Erroll took care of Darlene and incorporated her into their household and their daily routine. Kenzie later told Jan she first saw Darlene as unwanted work and expense, but grew to love her. She gave more attention to her than even Erroll did. Darlene didn't walk without help, didn't talk at all, and didn't interact with them in any way, so except for her physical needs, she didn't demand attention. The Patersons could always have privacy, because Darlene spent most of her time in bed or in a chair in the living room, and never went upstairs or outside. They didn't want to leave her alone in the house for more than a few minutes, however, so they couldn't both leave the home at the same time. Erroll usually stayed home from church with Darlene, so Kenzie could be the one to attend church, and to then spend Sunday afternoon at Cecelia's house.

The Paterson's second year on the farm proved easier than the first. Kenzie's business grew; even though she hired Mary Miller to help her two afternoons a week, she often had a backlog of work. She and Erroll made their first farm payment in full and on time, then made a payment and a half when the second was due. They not only made their farm payment, they bought a feather tick mattress and some blankets for the upstairs bed, plus sheets for the downstairs bed before the second winter. Erroll achieved excellent gardening results during their second summer, and they enjoyed more and better produce than they thought probably the McCartys in Scotland did. Erroll also traded a Shorthorn heifer for a Jersey heifer during the second summer. He told Kenzie the Jersey would give more and richer milk than a Shorthorn, so they'd eventually have more milk, cream, and butter, and he expected abundant food.

Erroll improved poultry performance as well as dairy production. He traded his banty rooster for a Leghorn, back during the first fall on the farm. He allowed several hens to set the following spring, and they produced six to eleven chicks each; he replaced all the pure banty hens that year with half banty/half Leghorn hens. He initiated another food-related project as well, when he saved seeds to start fruit trees in jars in the house, and by his second fall on the farm, had eight little tree seedlings in jars, ready to set out in a corner of the hay field when spring came.

Erroll stayed in the house on a rainy September morning in 1913, and engaged in his usual joking and teasing with Kenzie. "How many apple pies you gonna make today?"

"Erroll, you know the answer—none. If you could behave yourself for more than two minutes in a row, I might reward you, but as it stands now, none."

"You plan to look at cows this morning, while I do the easy stuff, like help Darlene with her breakfast, launder clothes, and what not?"

"Easy stuff! Easy stuff? You can walk around in a pasture a lot easier than I can do real work!"

"Maybe you need real work. Look, you're fat." He grinned and poked her in the side.

Kenzie burst into a laughing spell and couldn't stop for several seconds. When she did stop, her words rushed out. "I wondered when you'd notice—I'm so excited—I'm pregnant!"

"Wow!" Erroll's eyes widened, and he struggled to speak. "Are you sure?"

"Quite sure."

"Does Jan know?"

"Nobody knows."

"You need to tell Jan, so she can help you when the time comes."

"I'm pretty sure she'll see for herself. I'll begin a maternity dress Friday afternoon, and that'll probably tell her."

"Do you need anything? Like a crib or something?"

"Yes, it'll be wonderful if you can make a crib. And I'll make a few little baby dresses."

"How do you know the baby'll be a girl?"

"Erroll! All babies wear dresses, even boys."

"I didn't."

"Do you remember? I bet you wore them."

"I bet I didn't."

"We might as well stop talking about bets, because nobody still alive knows."

"You're right about that—if not about much else. Looks like the rain stopped; I gotta begin chores."

"Yes, Erroll, you're right about that last, if not about anything else!"

Erroll did his morning chores, entered the barn to pick up his one-man saw, walked down by the creek, and cut down a dead ash tree. He sawed the trunk into three lengths he planned to use for a crib, including the longest, then judged it might be about noon. He returned to the house, where Kenzie had a hearty lunch ready. He commented on the meal and on their current life. "Did you think we'd ever have it made like we do now, back when we walked to Glasgow?"

"No, no more than you did."

"Why didn't you tell me about the baby before today?"

"I wanted to be sure, and then I waited for you to notice."

"Do you still want to adopt a baby?"

"No, but it'll be wonderful if we have another one—or six—after this first one."

"Have you thought of a name?"

"Of course. Have you?"

"How could I? I didn't know anything about a baby until this morning. What name did you think of?"

"I have two. MacKenzie if a girl or Laren if a boy. Do those sound all right to you?"

"Perfect." Erroll paused, then changed the subject. "How's Darlene today?"

"Just the same, as nearly as I can tell."

"Good." He changed the subject again. "I cut a seasoned ash tree today, even though I have some green wood on a new wood pile behind the house. I don't have anything long enough for a crib already up here, but I'll split the ash and put the parts I need in the barn this afternoon."

"Wonderful, Erroll. I need to work on a couple coats and some pants. I'll finish those today, and will probably ask you to deliver them in Rounder tomorrow."

"Yeah, they'll be no problem if you want'em to go to Rounder."

They finished their lunch and Erroll went out to work on crib parts. He finished the crib near the end of February, well before Kenzie woke him before dawn on Thursday, March 15, 1914. "I think the baby's about to come, Erroll. Go get Jan."

Jan said Erroll nearly broke her door down with his violent knock that morning. Both Jan and Erroll returned quickly, whereupon Jan banished Erroll from the upstairs of the house. He heard a cry shortly after sunrise, and only a few minutes later Jan came down the stairs with the baby. She said Kenzie had an easy time, although Kenzie argued she didn't. Jan said the baby's name was Laren Kenneth Paterson, and she'd stay all day. She asked Erroll to go explain to Ron, and he went out the door instantly. Baby Laren often played on the floor by Darlene's feet when he grew, and he appeared to like her.

Kenzie realized she loved Darlene, and talked to Erroll about her during breakfast one day. "Erroll, sometimes I avoid stupid mistakes only because you won't let me make them. Like when I wanted to give up during our walk to Glasgow, or more recently, when I wanted to leave Darlene in Rochester. I'm glad you didn't let me do either."

"The last time you talked to me like that, you threatened to kiss me."

"I didn't just threaten, I did it. And I'm fixin' to do it again."

"Kenzie! Right in the next room from Darlene and Laren?"

"Right in front of Darlene, Laren, or anybody else who might want to look. Be ready, because here I come." Erroll allowed Kenzie to victimize him yet again, so much he left the house late enough to check the mailbox.

He came back in the house after only a couple minutes. "Kenzie, we have another notice about a registered letter at the post office. It's addressed to me this time."

"Aha. What'll you do about it?"

"Well, I'll go to the post office to see what it is. I'll go today after I finish my chores." When he made it to Rounder, he picked up an envelope at the post office, but didn't open it until after he returned.

He found Kenzie in the living room feeding Darlene when he entered the house. She demanded, "Tell me what it is."

"I haven't opened it yet."

"Open it and read it."

Erroll opened the envelope. "It's long."

"Read it."

A letterhead identified the letter as something from a UK Probate Court. He didn't read that part to Kenzie, only the body of the letter, and he read, "We believe you're the only surviving heir to the Arthur McCarty estate. A Mr. Rex Smalley posed as Eric McCarty during and after a long string of poisonings. Mr. Smalley first murdered Eric McCarty and assumed his identity in France in late 1879, then murdered Arthur McCarty in early 1880. An unknown number of years later, he murdered his wife, the mother of his young son Dal, and even later during the early 1900's, murdered one of the McCarty estate employees. Polis arrested his son, Dal, in North Ballachulish in 1912 for public drunkenness and brawling, and he subsequently implicated Mr. Smalley in the earlier murders. Dal died in jail; an autopsy found poison. A court convicted Mr. Smalley of all the murders, and he is presently in a lunatic asylum in the south of the country. The estate is appraised at 1 to 1.5 million pounds sterling. Court administration continues, but you may take possession when you arrive."

Erroll stopped reading. Both he and Kenzie sat in stunned silence, as Kenzie interrupted Darlene's breakfast. Erroll eventually reacted. "Wow!"

"Yes, that's all I can say, too. Wow!"

"I don't want to go back to the UK, or to try to operate an estate after all the progress we've made here, and the good friends we have. How do you feel about it, Kenzie?"

"Me either."

"Do you suppose we can sell it?"

"Maybe the court will sell it, Erroll. How can we find out what options we have?"

"Hoo-oo, my, Kenzie. Can we merely write back and ask?"

"That should work. I realize you just returned from Rounder, but would your letter go out faster if you mail it from the post office?"

"Probably. I'll write fast, and get started fast. Do you think Darlene's ready for more breakfast?"

"Oh, yeah. I almost forgot what I'm about here."

Erroll wrote a short letter, addressed an envelope, went upstairs for money, and headed for the post office. He bought the needed postage at the post office, plus another dime's worth of two-cent stamps, and mailed the letter. He came back home in time for lunch.

Kenzie speculated during the meal, "Do you suppose the court can merely put up a 'For Sale' sign?"

"I don't know, Kenzie. We have to wait to see what they say."

"Do you realize, Erroll, that one, to one and a half million pounds, is equivalent to almost five to over seven million dollars?"

"I knew it was big, but I didn't multiply it all out."

"I did, and you're right—it's big."

Time barely moved, and the Patersons checked their mailbox often until the court's reply to Erroll showed up. Kenzie insisted he open and read it immediately, and he needed no persuasion. The letter said they could return and take possession, or sell the estate. The court estimated it could take up to a year to sell an estate that large. Kenzie reacted first. "We have another decision to make."

"I thought we already decided we don't want to go back."

"We did. But what will we do with all that money?"

"You know, Kenzie, I didn't even think about that, but we'll be in the clover. We can pay off the farm, buy the bed for Laren he'll need soon, and maybe even put in one of those telephones like Ron has. We'll stuff more in our envelope upstairs than we can ever spend."

"I don't know if we should spend it, Erroll. It's bad money. Maybe we should give it away."

"What?"

"People helped us before we came here, when they couldn't afford to do it. Maybe we should help them back."

"We're about to have a bunch of money. Money's neither good nor bad, Kenzie, and it doesn't know where it came from. We can help people and spend plenty as well."

"I don't think it's ours to spend, not any of it. Do you think we should at least pray about it a couple days before we decide?"

"Whatever you think Kenzie, but what happened to your big goal to pay for the farm?"

"It's not my goal, Erroll, it's our goal. Isn't it?"

"Of course it is, and we can do it now."

"It's bad money Erroll. We'll do it the slow but sure way, with good money. We still need to pray about it."

Chapter 10
1915 – 1920

The Patersons prayed about the money, and also continued to talk. Kenzie suggested places to get advice. "I know one of us must always be home with Laren and Darlene, but maybe we can separately talk to Pastor Nick, and later to Conrad Decker the lawyer. If we decide to give back, Decker might know how best to do it."

"Any of that's all right with me, Kenzie. If you want to go see Pastor Nick first, I'll stay here. But you shouldn't just show up. Maybe you ought to wait until Sunday, and then ask him for a time that he likes."

"Yeah, perhaps. I'll ask for two times, one for each of us."

"Great, Kenzie."

Kenzie talked first to Pastor Nick, and reported back. "He didn't help. He bent over backward to stay out of it, and wouldn't come down on either side. I still think we should keep our hands off the money."

Erroll went to see Pastor Nick a day later, and he too came away with an unchanged opinion. He and Kenzie talked more. "Kenzie, I can go along with sending part of our money back to other people, but to send all of it seems extreme; wrong for us, wrong for Laren, and wrong for Darlene."

"Perhaps we can do an Erroll thing and say we don't have to decide today. We can ask the court to sell the estate. They wrote it could take up to a year, so we'll have that much time to decide. We truly don't have to decide today, and in the meantime, we can talk to Cecelia and to Ron and Jan to see what they think."

"I know what they'll say. They'll say your notion is bad for us."

"Do you mind if I ask them about it?"

"Do you really want to advertise we're about to be rich, Kenzie?"

"Perhaps not, but if we do it your way, people will know. How about if I check it out with the entire group at Cecelia's on Sunday?"

"We're going to decide, regardless of what they say. What difference does their opinion make?"

"Perhaps their opinion doesn't matter to us, Erroll, but their reasons might."

"Whatever. Call me stubborn if you want to, but I won't change. And I know Cecelia's bunch will say I'm right."

"We do agree we want the court to sell the estate, don't we? Can we write the letter to ask them to do that?"

"Of course, Kenzie. Will you write it?"

"Yes, I'll write it today, if you don't think today's too soon."

"No, today's fine Kenzie." They talked more about what to say in the letter, and decided the letter should begin with a thank you sentence, and end with a second sentence to ask the court to sell the estate. Kenzie wrote it that way, and Erroll took it to the mailbox the same day. A letter from the court came back in a couple weeks, but it merely acknowledged the Patersons' request, and stated they would soon put the estate on the market.

They dropped the debate about money for a while, but later in the summer faced a more immediate crisis. Kenzie went to the door of the house and screamed for Erroll just after lunch. Erroll ran toward her, responding more to the tone of her voice than to her words. "Is Laren with you, Erroll?"

"No, isn't he in the house?"

"No. I've looked upstairs and down. He's not here, Erroll." Panic filled her voice.

"You stay with Darlene. I'll look."

Kenzie yelled again after several minutes. "Go ask Jan if she'll stay with Darlene. I'll help you look." Erroll ran across the road, asked, and both Jan and Ron came. Jan stayed with Darlene, and Ron helped with the search. They scoured the farm from north to south and east to west. They looked in the pond, the barn, the cellar, and with fore-boding, in the well, but found nothing. Kenzie began to cry; Erroll stopped searching to try to comfort her. Between sobs Kenzie asked, "Did you look in the barn?"

"Yes, Kenzie, we did. All through it."

"Did you look in the loft?"

"No, but Laren can't climb the ladder."

"Let's go look anyway."

They went, while Ron checked the pond again. They ran back out of the barn with Laren in Kenzie's arms. She shouted, "We found him asleep on the hay in the loft, Ron! He's all right!" Kenzie cried for an hour, and she hugged Laren nearly twice that long. She took him in the house to show Jan, and to thank her for her help. Jan hugged Kenzie and Laren together.

Kenzie exulted to Darlene, "We found him! He was only asleep!" even though Darlene didn't respond and gave no evidence she under-stood.

Erroll didn't agree with Kenzie about the estate money, but she remained adamant. He eventually faked agreement to take away her reason to talk to Cecelia, and thus to the world, and to have a plan—any plan. The mailman dropped another notice about a registered let-ter in their mailbox a couple weeks before Laren's second birthday. Erroll went to the post office and returned with an envelope from the UK court. Kenzie demanded he open it immediately, and as before, he did. The envelope contained a check for $5,824,506.18.

Kenzie hugged Erroll, and exclaimed, "Wonderful! Do you have a list of people about to receive money?"

"No."

"I do. How about something like this: two million divided equally among employees, or heirs of deceased employees of the McCarty estate—not including employees of the dress shops—from 1887 to the present, plus the People Feeder Group in St. Louis. And then we use whatever remains after we pay Conrad Decker to set it all up, to make twelve equal monthly payments to Tiny Kirk Food Wagon Ministry, to Mr. and Mrs. Ed McDowell in Invermoriston, to Mr. and Mrs. James Bradley at North Ballachulish, and to Thelma and Burt Bradley by Loch Leven?"

"That list sounds good as any to me, Kenzie. Every one of those people or groups helped us when we really needed it." Erroll asked Kenzie to write the list, and then he took it to Rounder to see Conrad Decker.

Attorney Decker looked at the list. "I don't see any reason we can't do this, Mr. Paterson. The only suggestion I might make is that you invest the money for the second group, make grants to them in perpetuity, and include their heirs. You'll need to set up a trust. I can ask Rounder Bank to handle the details for that part. The trust can also make the immediate payments your list describes."

"That sounds good to me, Mr. Decker. What should I do now?"

"Nothing at all. Let me arrange the legal matters, then you can take the check to the bank and endorse it over to the trust."

"How much time do you need?"

"Maybe about a week." The lawyer did his thing, payments went out, and the Patersons received numerous thank you notes and tales of extreme need. Thelma Bradley wrote a two-page letter and reported Burt died a year earlier. She wrote that James tried to look in on her occasionally, but had to walk three hours each way to do it, and she feared for a time she wouldn't survive. But she said the Paterson money would enable her to move to North Ballachulish, would finance a comfortable life for her, and would allow her to establish a savings account. She expected to be fine. Pastor MacIntire at Tiny Kirk wrote to say the added money gave the kirk means to make three wagon trips per summer, instead of one, and further enabled them to take two wagons per trip.

The letters impressed Erroll, and he apologized to Kenzie. "Do you remember when we argued about some things, we did them my way, and you later told me my way worked better?"

"I sure do, Erroll."

"We handled the estate money your way, and I have to say your way worked better."

"Yes?"

"Yes what, Kenzie?"

"Do you remember what I did next, after I said your way worked better?"

"You kissed me. So please don't run, Kenzie—I'm going to kiss you!"

"I won't even pretend to run. Get over here." Erroll kissed Kenzie repeatedly, and tried to kiss last, but didn't succeed, even though he continued to try for several minutes.

After Erroll conceded defeat in his effort to be last, they returned to their talk. "We shouldn't tell anyone we ever had McCarty money or that we gave it away, you agree, Kenzie?"

"Believe it or not, Erroll, I agree with you about that. We're lucky that people accepted the money, and we must not merely refuse to talk about it, we must forget it if we can."

"Right."

The Patersons prospered in a smaller way on their own after they gave away the estate money. The Jersey heifer freshened. Erroll fenced off a small pasture around the barn for the Jersey and two Shorthorn cows, and kept their calves in the barn. He allowed all three calves to nurse one of the Shorthorns, and kept the milk from the Jersey and the other Shorthorn. He walked into Rounder every day to sell dairy products at Jake County Grocery, and he and Kenzie, as well as Ron and Jan, had all the milk, cream, and butter they wanted.

The world war began in 1914 before Laren's first birthday. Erroll had to register for the military draft toward the end of the war, and later actually appeared before the Jake County Draft Board, but they exempted him from the draft on two counts; he worked in the 'essential' agriculture industry, and he supported a dependent parent--not his own parent, but Kenzie's. By the end of the war, eight little fruit trees grew in a corner of the hay field. He never did take a second crop off the hay field, but continued to herd his cows in it in winter, the same as he did the first winter.

The water gap at the lower end of the creek—Rocky Bottom Creek—washed out during the summer of 1914, and Ben Jones's land bordered Paterson land on three sides by then. Brush from the water gap settled on the Jones farm, and Ben sued the Patersons for damage the brush supposedly caused. Conrad Decker recommended they settle out of court for a payment of $600. They gained a half-year on their farm payment before they settled with Ben, but the incident cost so much they struggled to get back to even on the 1915 payment.

Erroll traded a barren cow to Rob Mercer for a young filly in 1914—Kenzie dubbed her Robin—and used her to pull the buggy. Both he and Kenzie stopped walking to Rounder after they had Robin, and their material comfort continued to improve, despite Ben Jones.

As the Paterson's fortunes advanced, however, the Cline's receded. Ron's arthritis gradually worsened and forced him to rely ever more on his cane. Jan came to the house to see Erroll on a December morning in 1915. "Ron'd whack me up-side the head if he knew why I came over here, but will you cut ice for him this winter?"

"Of course I will. I'll start today."

"I'm so grateful. I'm afraid he'll slip and break a bone."

Erroll grinned and looked at Kenzie. "I wonder if Kenzie worries that I'll break a bone?"

Kenzie grinned too. "You're so tough and strong, I have complete confidence in you. And besides, you can't break a bone, because Laren and Darlene need you, almost as much as I do."

Jan crowded another request among the Paterson jokes. "Will you dream up a yarn about why you'll cut ice this winter? Please don't tell Ron I have anything to do it."

"Yeah, I'll take all the blame. I'll tell him, truthfully, I think he's too unsteady to be out where nobody can hear him if he calls." Erroll cut ice for Ron that winter, and every winter thereafter, as long as Ron lived.

Erroll and Kenzie made their last farm payment to Cecelia two years early, on June 28, 1920, when their son Laren was six years old. Erroll brought up an old subject with Kenzie. "You said you wanted to adopt a baby when we paid the farm off, but then you said otherwise when you were expecting Laren. Do you still want to adopt?"

"Of course not, Erroll. We have Laren now."

"I didn't know if that mattered."

"Do you remember why I said I wanted to adopt a baby?"

"No, I think I do well to remember the fact, and could care less about the reason."

"I said I wanted someone to remember us, to carry on, and to build on what we've done."

"Give me a couple minutes and I'll forget again, Kenzie."

"Don't laugh, Erroll. We still need that. We did really good to pay for the farm, but we can't relax now; we need to accumulate an inheritance for Laren, so he doesn't have to start from zero the way we did."

"Whatever you say, Kenzie, but we'll have more money to spend now."

"No, Erroll, we need to be as careful as always, and to save as much as we can, not only for Laren, but for unexpected problems."

"Why earn money if we don't spend it Kenzie?"

"Do you remember our last months in Scotland?"

Erroll grinned. "How could I forget?"

"Extra money would've been nice, don't you think?'

"You can always think of a special case, but it doesn't matter, because we got 'er made now, Kenzie." Kenzie didn't answer.

Chapter 11
1920 - 1936

Laren's attraction to Darlene continued and increased. He could talk to her whenever he wanted, and she never interrupted him. He talked to her often, and sometimes at length, even though she didn't respond and probably didn't realize he spoke to her.

Erroll enrolled Laren in Jake County Number Five Elementary School the same year he and Kenzie made the last farm payment. Local people referred to the school simply as Number Five. Laren's first teacher was Miss Bonnie Chrisman. Erroll's father home-schooled both Erroll and Kenzie, so they appreciated the luxury of a formal school for Laren; they lived barely over a half-mile from the school, but Rose Miller, daughter of Emmanuel and Mary, walked an even shorter distance than Laren. She lived across the Jones driveway from the school, and completed first grade a year before Laren entered school.

Laren quickly adjusted to school, but adjusted only slowly, if at all, when Darlene died in January during his second year. He received the news one day when he came home from school. Erroll and Kenzie lingered at breakfast in the kitchen that day, and heard an unfamiliar sound. Kenzie went to look, and then screamed, "Come in here, Erroll!"

Erroll ran and found Kenzie clutching Darlene's arm. "What is it Kenzie?"

"I think Darlene's gone. She threw up on the bed, and now she doesn't move."

"Should I ask Jan to call a doctor?"

"I think it's too late, Erroll. What do you think?"

Erroll looked at the uncharacteristic color of Darlene's face, touched her neck, and affirmed, "Yes, it's too late. Did she act different yesterday?"

"No, this happened out of the blue."

"I don't—do you know what we should do?"

"No, Erroll, this is a huge shock. Can we just sit here a minute?"

"We can if you want to, Kenzie."

They sat silently beside Darlene for several minutes before Kenzie pulled herself together. "Perhaps you should hitch up Robin. I'll clean the bed and we can both go to the funeral home in Rounder. Laren won't be home until after four, so we have as much time as we need."

They went to Rounder, the undertaker sent a wagon and empty pine box, and hauled Darlene away before Laren returned from school. He cried, and several times begged his parents to tell him where Darlene went. He didn't sleep soundly that night, and Kenzie got up with him several times. He said he didn't feel like going to school the next day, and Kenzie didn't make him do it. On the following day, Saturday, all three Patersons rode the buggy to town to see Pastor Nick about a funeral, and after they consulted with the undertaker, chose a time on Sunday afternoon, with burial to be in Rounder Cemetery. Laren recovered slightly Saturday, but the funeral set him off again.

When the funeral ended and the Patersons went home, Kenzie talked about Darlene. "Erroll, I'm so glad Darlene came to live with us, and didn't die an unknown pauper in Rochester. I hate that she's gone, but it's far better than it would otherwise be."

"I agree, Kenzie. I'm not sure status counts for anything after death, but she definitely had more of it before death than if she'd stayed in Rochester. She may have been the last of our parents, unless your dad still walks around in Kentucky, or wherever. Do you know how old he is?"

"Not a clue, but your mom would only be in her sixties, and Poppa in his seventies. My dad could possibly be alive someplace."

"Do you want to try to find him?"

"If he wanted to find me, Erroll, it'd be easy, so I think he didn't look. If he didn't want to find me, I don't want to find him."

"Me either. Do you remember anything at all about Rochester?"

"Not much. I can't remember Poppa's house at all. Can you?"

"I can visualize a backyard scene, that's all. But we need to think about Laren; where is he?"

"He's in the middle of Darlene's bed, Erroll, but at least he isn't crying."

"We need to talk to him."

They went from the kitchen to the living room. Erroll implored, "You wanta go out and help me with the chores tonight?"

Laren looked unusually solemn. "No, I want to sit here all night."

"You can't sit there all night, Son. You have your own bed upstairs now. Momma and I will have to take this bed out of the house, and maybe sell it if we can. You sure you don't want to go help me with the chores? You'll feel better if you do."

"You won't take Darlene's bed away while we're outside, will you?"

"No, Son. We might do it Monday while you're at school."

"Then I won't go to school Monday."

"If we do it then, it won't be because you're at school, but because it's time to do it. If we take Darlene's bed out, it will mean nobody will ever come here to take her place; you don't want anybody to do that do you?"

"No. Do I have to go out and help you tonight?"

"You'll feel better if you do."

"I don't want to feel better. I want Darlene back."

"She's not coming back, Son. Let's go out now." Laren went out with Erroll to do the evening chores. Erroll walked with him to school Monday, but he didn't get his little boy exuberance back for several weeks, and it took as long for Erroll and Kenzie to recover as it did for Laren.

Kenzie's sewing business, Erroll's cattle, garden, chickens, orchard, and the general Paterson family situation grew and improved over the next few years, but the Cline condition continued the opposite way. Erroll first cut ice for Ron in December, 1915, then added more of Ron's work as the years went by. He eventually bought Ron's horses and his hay equipment, and did all his work the two years before he died, on August 17, 1930. Ron and Jan had two sons in California, but neither came back for the funeral. Jan had a tough time for a while after Ron died, and Kenzie tried to support her for a couple months, but she bounced back. She rented her 120 acres to Erroll for 1931 and beyond, excluding the house and chicken house. She hid most of her money in her house, but lost about $150 in the 1931 run on Rounder Bank. She didn't move out of her house until the uncommonly hot summer of 1934 prompted her to leave the farm in March, 1935, when she had a farm sale and moved into a smaller house in Rounder. The Patersons did all right on the rented farm in 1935, but fed hay almost all summer in 1936, and culled their cattle herd at a loss because of the dry weather that summer.

Cecelia Shier's health broke later than Ron's, but deteriorated faster, and she died earlier. Erroll hitched Robin to the buggy almost every day in 1927 and 1928 for Kenzie to take food to Cecelia, until she died November 6, 1928. Cecelia had a daughter named Cindy in New York City, but Cindy could only visit sporadically. She, her husband Bart, and their three children came to Rounder for the funeral on the ninth, however.

Laren graduated from Number Five in 1928 and from Rounder High School in 1932; Rose Miller preceded him by a year, both times. Laren and Rose dated during high school, continued after they graduated, and married April 7, 1935. Rose's parents rented their house from Ben Jones for years, but Ben sold the eighty with their house in 1935, and they moved into Rounder in March, a week after Jan Cline moved.

Erroll and Kenzie helped both Jan and the Millers move. Kenzie talked somberly the evening after they helped the Millers. "Do you realize, Erroll, we're fifty-three years old, only a year younger than Poppa was when he died?"

"Yeah, and after helping the Millers all day, I feel every day of those years. Can you believe how much has happened since Poppa died?"

"Yes, maybe it's time we slow down a bit, Erroll."

"For sure. Didn't you notice we already did it? We started to ease off when Laren graduated from high school. We do more on the farm now, but we couldn't without Laren. We're not as weak as Poppa in his fifty-third year, however. I don't think we'll kick the bucket as young as Poppa did."

"One of my biggest regrets is we left Poppa back by Inverness. Nobody will remember him when our generation's gone."

"Yeah, Kenzie, I worry about that too. But we need to cheer up. Let's plan a move into Jan's house."

"Planning another move isn't exactly cheerful, Erroll."

"I tried. You know anything more cheerful?"

"We can have apple pie for supper."

"Now that's cheerful. How soon can we start?"

"Unless you want more than pie for supper, we can start as soon as I cut it."

"Really cheerful. Let's do it."

Because Jan's farm house contained more, bigger, and nicer rooms than the Paterson house, because Erroll and Kenzie already rented her house as part of her farm, and because about-to-be-newlyweds Laren and Rose would soon need a place to live, Erroll and Kenzie moved across the road to Jan's house a couple weeks after the Millers moved. Laren remained in the old house to look after livestock, and married Rose a little less than a week later. Kenzie not only didn't resume Jan's Friday sewing bees when they moved, she turned her seamstress business over to her long-time helper, Mary Miller, Rose's mother.

Kenzie turned philosopher again on the evening after Laren's wedding. "You slowed down when Laren graduated, Erroll. Now it's my turn. Laren's wedding took a lot out of me, but it's over, and my life should settle down to match yours."

"Yep, we have it made, don't we?"

"Erroll, I wish you wouldn't say we have it made."

"I gotta be right this time. What can go wrong now, at this late stage of our lives?"

"I don't know, Erroll, but please don't say it."

"All right, I take it back. Can I do anything else for you?"

"You know what I mean. Let's sit back and enjoy a quiet evening."

"I might be for that, depending on what you mean by quiet."

"I don't mean we doze off at seven, if that's your drift."

"Good. Maybe we can do something semi-quiet, like let me chase you around the farm a couple times."

"Behave yourself, Erroll."

"I don't want to be that quiet."

"Hush. Be still. Be utterly quiet."

"I will for now, but do you know what happens when you boil water in a sealed can?"

"I'll risk it, Erroll. I know how to deal with you when you get unruly."

"Can you name a time when I got unruly?"

"I can name hundreds, but I might miss one, and besides, I don't want to talk all night."

"That's a first!"

"Hush, Erroll. If anybody talks, it'll be me!"

"So what else is new?"

"You're nothing but talk. Stop doing it."

"You win, Kenzie. You out-talked me, and I quit."

"It's about time."

Rose's older sister Ellen and her husband Arthur died in a car wreck near Guymon, Oklahoma, on 'Black Sunday' during the 1935 dust storm there, exactly a week after Laren and Rose married. Ellen and Arthur left a fifteen-year-old son Baird, so Rose and Laren persuaded one of their former RHS classmates to drive them to Oklahoma and back. They brought Baird home with them and legally adopted him as soon as they could. Baird and his entire new family struggled with the change he brought, partly because of his age, only six years younger than Laren. They went through a lengthy adjustment period that troubled Baird more than anyone. "Do I have to call you Mom and Dad?"

Rose replied, "You don't have to, but we'll be thrilled if you do. Do you prefer different names?"

"Not really, but I already have a mom and dad."

Laren assured Baird, "We understand, and we for sure realize we'll never be Arthur and Ellen. But we want to do everything for you they would have done. What you call us is irrelevant to us and for you to decide."

"I'm grateful you brought me here—I mean I didn't have a job or anything—but my friends are all in Oklahoma. I'll probably never find another friend way out here in the wilderness."

"You might like adult friends too. Maybe Rose and I can do double duty and be friends as well as parents. And you'll love your grandparents, Emmanuel and Mary, and Erroll and Kenzie, I guarantee you will."

"I don't buy it, but I'm grateful to you, and I'll try to show it."

The newly formed Paterson family didn't gel for several weeks, but they formed a solid connection when they succeeded. Baird achieved, despite being skinny and short. He entered Rounder High School as a sophomore in the fall of 1935, earned good grades there, and won a partial scholarship to Avery Leiler University near the middle of Missouri.

Jan Cline died December 21, 1936. Neither of her sons from

California attended the funeral on the twenty-third, but on the twenty-eighth, her older son knocked on Erroll and Kenzie's door—the door to the house Jan had owned, and rented to the Patersons. Kenzie opened the door. "Yes?"

"Hello. I'm Kenneth Cline, Jan's son. May I come it?"

"Of course. My husband's here, and of course, come on in."

Kenneth entered and Kenzie took him through the kitchen to the front room. "Erroll, this is Kenneth Cline, Jan's boy. Kenneth, this is Erroll Paterson, my husband."

Kenneth ignored Kenzie after he met Erroll. "I'm glad to meet you, Mr. Paterson. The old place looks very much like it did when I grew up here. I'm not happy to come to you like this, but my brother, Claude, and I need to sell Mom's farm. We'll wait for it to go through probate, and then maybe in a year, we'll need you to either pay our price for it or move."

Chapter 12
1936 - 1937

Erroll stalled. "Do you have a place to stay in Rounder? Can we talk about our response for a few days?"

"I must start back this afternoon, but you can mail your answer to me. I have a shoe store in Santa Barbara. Here's my business card." Kenneth tossed a card at Erroll.

"How much do you want for the farm?"

"We must have $50 an acre, which is $6,000 for the entire 120."

"You'll never get fifty. The house'll sit vacant, the farm'll lay idle while you wait for it, and the value'll go down. You'll never get that much."

"That's our price. We'll look for your answer within two weeks. Good day."

"Good day to you. Have a safe trip back. Did you drive a car over the mountains?"

"No, that's Mom's car outside. I came to Rounder by train." Kenneth slammed the door as he went out.

Kenzie and Erroll watched Kenneth turn the car around and turn north toward Rounder. Then Kenzie asked, "What will we do? Laren and Rose live in our old house. What will we do?"

"How much do we have in the envelope in the kitchen?"

"We have just a few dollars over 4,300."

"Hmm. Thirty-five an acre works out to 4,200. Even that much might be a little high, but it's closer to today's land market than fifty. We need to talk to Laren and Rose, but Kenneth came all the way back here just to ask for money, so maybe he really needs it. I think there's a chance he'll jump at thirty-five. We'll have to move to Rounder if he doesn't, and I'll have to commute to the farm each day. If we don't buy the 120, we have to find a way to make eighty acres support two families, and it'll be tough. We'll have to do some things different, that's for sure."

"Let's don't be rash about spending our money, Erroll. We want to leave it to Laren and Rose as their inheritance. And they may want to pay college costs for Baird someday."

"Maybe we can build back up some. But even if we don't, the cash for the farm should be a fair exchange for us now, and for Laren and Rose later. We need to talk to them."

"I agree with one thing, Erroll, and that is we need to talk to the kids."

"For sure."

After lunch that same day they walked across the road to see Laren and Rose. Baird sat in, because of Rounder High's Christmas break, but didn't participate in the conversation with his grandparents. Kenzie outlined the situation. "A man who claims to be Kenneth Cline, Jan and Ron's boy, came out to see us this morning. He wants to sell Jan's farm and says we must either buy it or move in a year. After he left, we talked about doing both, but you're involved too, and we want to know what you think."

Laren inquired, "How much's 'e want?"

Erroll answered, "He wants $6,000 but the most we want to pay is $4,200."

"How much are those per acre?" Rose pulled a pencil and paper out of the drawer under the table in the living room.

Kenzie answered Rose. "Erroll figured those at fifty and thirty-five."

Rose raised her voice. "Ben Jones only got thirty for the place my family lived on. I think that's all the Kenneth guy should get. The Jones place has a house on it, same as the Cline farm."

"I agree, Rose, but Erroll thinks we should offer $4200. That's almost all we have, and if we spend that, we'll have nothing left for you and Laren to inherit."

Laren reacted, to Kenzie, as well as to Kenneth. "Inheritance doesn't matter, but do you mean Kenneth couldn't come here for his mom's funeral, but could come to dun you for money? That stinks."

Kenzie responded, "Yes, it stinks, but it doesn't have anything to do with the decision we need to make—except if the guy's character is suspect, we need to be sure he can't challenge us legally if we make an offer."

Rose replied, "You're right, and I think you should buy the farm or not, based on what you think, without regard for what we might think."

Erroll said, "We're a two-family farm, and both our individual savings and our available land matter to both families. We don't want to decide either way without your input."

Rose asked. "What will you do if you have to move?"

Erroll waited a moment to answer. "We can move to Rounder, but that'll cost money too, and we'll only have eighty acres for our cattle."

Rose replied, "A move's second-best. You should offer the guy $4200—not a penny more—and hope he takes it." She paused. "What do you think, Laren?"

"I don't know how we'll make it without that extra 120. I don't care about the money myself," he looked at Kenzie, "but I know it's important to you. In the end, it's your money and up to you to decide, but I'll sure back you if you decide to buy the farm. I think that can work out better in the long run."

Erroll nodded. "That's the way I feel about it. I say we write a letter to Kenneth, offer $4200, all four of us sign it, and then we mail it tomorrow."

"Well, I suppose I agree."

Rose wrapped it up. "Since Momma agrees, and I do, that makes four. Who'll write the letter?"

Erroll looked at Rose and suggested, "How about you?"

"I think you should write the letter, since you have the money."

Erroll agreed to do it, borrowed Rose's pencil and paper, and wrote a letter immediately. All four signed it, Laren put it an envelope, addressed it to the location shown on the business card, and promised to stamp it and put it in the mailbox in the morning. Erroll received a letter from Kenneth eight days later, instructing him to send $4200, with a promise of a deed in about a year.

Kenzie read the letter. "Erroll, can you see fire shoot out of my ears?"

"I sure can, Dear. I know what fire looks like when it shoots out of there."

"It isn't funny, Erroll. If you send that money, we'll never see a deed. You can bet your bottom dollar on it, and if we do what Kenneth wants, we'll be pretty close to that last one."

"What do you suggest we do instead?"

"I suggest we take this letter straight to Conrad Decker and see what he says."

"Actually, I agree with you, Kenzie. I don't wanta send money to Kenneth under almost any circumstance. When do you want to go?"

"How about tomorrow?"

"Fine. I'll hitch Robin as soon as I do my morning chores."

The Patersons went to Attorney Decker's office, showed him the letter, and explained the background. Conrad smiled and suggested, "Why don't you have a seat, leave this letter with me, and let me handle the whole thing? We won't need your money for a while yet. I'll—"

Kenzie interrupted, "That's what I thought. That Kenneth is—"

Conrad broke back in. "Yes, the entire situation is a problem, but I can handle it. I'll let you know when it's all resolved, and when we need your money. Please know I appreciate your confidence in my work."

Erroll stood and shook Conrad's hand. "Thank you, Mr. Decker. Do you have an idea about when you'll need the money?"

"Probably about a year. I'll let you know."

"Thanks again. Are we done here?"

"Yes I think we are, at least for now."

The Patersons left Conrad's office, went out to their buggy, and drove home.

Rose and Laren had a second son, McLaren Arthur Paterson, born April 22, 1937, at Jakesville Hospital in Jakesville. Baird completed his junior year at RHS about a month after McLaren's birth, and bragged about his new brother. Only his grandparents were prouder. Kenzie raved, "Isn't he cute? We're counting on Laren to build on our success, and there's no way to guess how high Baird and McLaren will fly."

Conrad rang up the Patersons in February after McLaren's birth, and told Kenzie they could complete the land purchase any time, and should bring the money. They went to the attorney's office the next day, gave Conrad the money, and received a deed needing only their own signatures, which Conrad witnessed. They owned eighty acres the day before, but now, two hundred total.

The poverty days across the water receded to a far distant past; Erroll grinned and commented about it. "You remember I once predicted we'd be the McCartys of Missouri? You think we're close?"

"I certainly hope not, Erroll. Put your mind on more constructive stuff."

"You know what I mean, Kenzie."

"Yes, I do, and I wouldn't trade our situation now for the McCarty's situation then, not in a million years. But we're pretty ordinary here, not the richest people around like the McCartys were. Now that we bought 120 acres, I think we should buy a smaller amount in Rounder Cemetery."

"What are you talking about, Kenzie?"

"We need to buy a cemetery plot for ourselves, so Laren and Rose won't have to do it someday."

"Kenzie, you're silly. You've wanted to kill us off for over forty years, and you're still at it."

"I'm not silly this time, Erroll. How many people as old as King Solomon do you see around here, or even as old as George Washington? We won't be the two shining exceptions and live forever, you know."

"How many times've you been wrong about our imminent deaths, Kenzie?"

"Maybe you're just a lucky charm, Erroll, or maybe God isn't ready for us to go. But your luck, or God's providence, won't keep us alive forever. Whatever it costs to buy a cemetery plot now is that much less Laren and Rose will have to spend later."

"I'm not interested in the slightest way, Kenzie, but if you want to check the cost, I suppose that's up to you." Kenzie bought a plot for the two of them the following week.

McLaren's early life was normal, ordinary, and unremarkable. His older brother, parents, and grandparents doted on him, and he may have thought he had dual residency, because he spent much time in his grandparents' home. The birth of another grandchild reinforced Kenzie's perception of advancing age, however. McLaren came along during their mid fifties, and started to school after they were sixty. Kenzie asked, "Erroll, do you know we're already older than Poppa was when he died?"

"Yes, I do. What can I do about it?"

"I mean we're old, and I, for one, can feel it. How about you?"

"Yep, I'm glad Laren's still young and can do most of the work . . . you once could run faster than me, but I bet you can't do it now."

"Oh, Erroll, I can too, but I'm too lazy to prove it."

"As Stan, back by Inverness, would say, 'Aye, right'."

"Talk all you want, but you're even older than I am."

"Aye, right. Two days."

"At our age, Erroll, that's significant."

"At my age, Kenzie, I'm too tired to argue with you. Maybe I'm more old and feeble than I thought."

"Eat your supper, Erroll, it'll put you to sleep."

Chapter 13
1938 - 1947

Back before Baird decided to go halfway across Missouri to college at Avery Leiler University in the fall of 1938, none of the Patersons saw need for a car. Then Rose and Laren bought a 1934 Ford Tudor Sedan to take him there and to go after him at Christmas and in the spring. Erroll and Kenzie sometimes borrowed the car, but more often they relied on the buggy and on successors to Robin they named Robin Two, and later, Robin Three.

The older Patersons slowed more than before. Soon after Baird entered college, Erroll relinquished almost all the heavy farm work to Laren, even though he continued to milk the four to five Jersey cows fresh at various times, and he continued to do the garden work for both families. Laren took over the beef cattle, chickens, orchard, and hay, and relegated Erroll to helper status in those enterprises. Erroll and Kenzie remained in the former Cline house west of the road, and moved the garden and Jerseys to the west side, while Laren and Rose lived in the original four room Paterson house on the east side.

McLaren moped when Baird left the farm for ALU. Baird worked hours to help McLaren learn to walk, and later adjusted his walking pace to accommodate McLaren's short legs; he went away to college before McLaren's second birthday, and McLaren didn't understand his absence. He learned to anticipate Baird's return for Christmas breaks and summer vacations as he grew older, and after initial shyness by both, they always revived their old camaraderie. Although McLaren eventually grew old enough to better understand Baird would return to college and why, he missed Baird for several days after each visit.

The Japanese bombed Pearl Harbor in 1941 during Baird's junior year at ALU. Laren talked about it. "I'm only thirty-seven years old, Rose, and I think I should volunteer."

"You don't think you're needed here? You might be gone for years, or worse, forever. I understand how you feel, but you need to use your head, Laren."

"You could say the same about almost everybody else in the army. I know it will be a sacrifice and a risk for us all, but I have to do it, Rose."

"Nonsense. You mean you want to do it—you don't have to do it."

"I don't like to do anything whatsoever without your agreement, but I have to do this."

"Before you do, will you talk to your Momma about it?"

"Sure, but I have to do it."

Laren talked to both his parents about the army. They understood his feeling, but argued against it. Much against their wishes, and especially against Rose's, Laren and Baird volunteered together. The draft board rejected Laren outright, because he worked in an industry essential to the war effort, and had a dependent child. Baird made it all the way to his army physical, but didn't go far into it, because neither his weight nor his height met minimum standards. Laren and Baird expressed disappointment, but Rose, Kenzie, and Erroll praised selective service judgment. Adults in the Paterson family and the Rounder area remained aware of the war effort and almost all participated in it, but McLaren knew little about it except that grownups talked about it a lot. He felt more impact when Baird started graduate school at ALU and didn't come home for the summer in 1942.

Rose accompanied McLaren to Number Five in the fall of 1943, and enrolled him in first grade. McLaren liked Miss Mattie Harvey, his teacher, and enthusiasm filled him for a couple weeks, but then a boy named Skip Barnes noticed him and annoyed him. Skip had age, weight, and height advantages over McLaren; he was the only second grade student in the school. McLaren didn't know why, but he affronted Skip, who ridiculed his name as a 'sissy name', and called him 'stuck up' because his parents farmed nearby and his mom sat on the school board. Skip's parents lived a couple miles southwest of the Patersons, but the Barnes and Paterson families were barely acquainted. Skip's father worked in an insurance office in Rounder and his mother taught third grade at Rounder Elementary.

The smaller McLaren tried to avoid the bigger Skip, but Skip pushed McLaren from behind, tripped him from the side, and blocked his way when he tried to walk. McLaren didn't retaliate, but continued to duck conflict.

Skip pushed McLaren one day while inside the schoolhouse, Miss Harvey saw it, and admonished, "Skip! That's not how we treat people in school!"

"I didn't mean to do it, Miss Harvey. I tripped on accident."

Miss Harvey adopted a disbelieving tone. "See that you don't have any more 'accidents' in this schoolhouse."

"Yes, Ma'am."

Skip blamed McLaren for Miss Harvey's reprimand, and accosted him later that same day, during recess outside the school. "You almost fell on your face, and you did it in front of Miss Harvey. I ought to beat you up for that."

McLaren turned to walk away. Skip yelled after him, "Walk away from me, will you, you little twerp. I'll show you how to walk away; I'll steer you right through that mud puddle." Skip pushed McLaren down in the mud puddle. McLaren forgot about his 'walk away' ethic, and came up fighting. Both boys went down in the puddle and covered themselves with mud; Skip rolled on top of McLaren, then stood up with his foot on him, and laughed at him. "You look like a mud ball. We should call you Muck, because you look like a muddy muck."

McLaren struggled to fight more, but Skip didn't let him up.

Skip continued to laugh and call him Muck, until McLaren gave in. "You can call me Muck, or whatever you want, if you let me up."

Skip took his foot off McLaren, but called him Muck from that time forward. The other students eventually called him that, and finally, even Miss Harvey did. His name changed to Muck. He remained McLaren at home, but became Muck everywhere else.

Skip bullied Muck all through that year, but the Barnes family moved out of the Number Five district into Rounder during the summer before school began again, and except for his moniker, Muck could forget about Skip for a while. Miss Harvey came back for Muck's second and third grades.

His parents traded their old Ford car for a used Chevy in 1945, three weeks before he began his third grade, but more importantly to Muck, Baird married Maye on the ALU campus in July of that year. Muck and his parents drove down for the ceremony and came back home the same day.

A new teacher, Mrs. Jesse Orlando, took over Number Five. She started with Muck's fourth grade and continued through his eighth. Muck didn't mind his early school years after Skip moved, but he saw electricity in his home as a bigger deal. The Rural Electrification Administration installed poles and wires down the east side of the road between the two Paterson houses during the summer and fall of 1946, and Kenzie and Erroll debated whether to 'hook on' to the new wires. Erroll argued, "We went all these years without it. We're old, and we'll probably never learn how to use it, so we might as well save the cost."

Kenzie disagreed. "Erroll, you don't have to work in a hot kitchen all summer. We can have an electric stove and never build a fire in the kitchen again. Our new laundry shed is nice, but you don't have to start the washer engine every week. The kerosene lamps work, sort of, but I've seen electric lights, and they make night like day. You're right about us being old, but that's all the more reason we need to keep up with progress."

"If that's what you think."

"That's what I think, Erroll, and that's only part of it. Rose needs it too. We should pay for ours, and pay for Rose's."

"Wait a minute, Kenzie. Do you have any idea what that will cost?"

"I don't care what it costs. We have the money, and Laren and Rose don't. They paid for Baird to go to college and now they need to save for McLaren to go. We're the people to do it, and Rose needs it."

"Let's at least check into what it will cost before we decide."

"I don't care when you decide, but I already decided. We'll do it, and after we do, you'll like it as well as anybody."

"Do you know, Kenzie, even as an old woman you look good when fire comes out of your ears that way."

"Don't laugh at me, Erroll. I intend to do it here, and across the road. Both."

"Fine, but we don't want to drop that on Laren out of the blue. I need to clear the way with him first."

"Clear all you want, but I'll ring up an electrician today."

Erroll tried to alert Laren, but found he and Rose already planned to hook on, so he asked Laren to talk to his momma about her plan to pay the cost. The elder Patersons paid, and electricity came on during a school day in October, soon after Muck began grade four. Everybody praised Kenzie's wisdom and generosity, even Erroll. Both Paterson houses had electric lights on day one, both families added electric cook stoves and electric irons within a week, and the following spring, electric refrigerators.

The next big event in Muck's life steered him toward an obsession. Mrs. Orlando presented a lesson about the forty-niners in California, and told how to pan for gold during a fifth grade social studies lesson. "The technique is to use a pan to scoop up gravel out of a stream bed, swirl it around a bit, then slowly pour out the water and gravel, leaving the heavier gold at the bottom of the pan."

Muck raised his hand and jerked it violently until Mrs. Orlando called on him. "Mrs. Orlando, this is practical! Do you need a special pan?"

"No, any pan will do. Something wide and shallow is best."

"Did anybody ever find gold in Missouri?"

"I've not heard about it, but can't rule it out."

"Do you think there's gold in Rocky Bottom Creek?"

"What's Rocky Bottom Creek?"

"It's a creek across the corner of our farm. Does it have gold in it?"

"I don't know about that creek, but anything's possible."

Muck ran the entire half-mile to his home after school that day, asked his mother for a pan, and ran on down the bluff to the creek. The creek didn't have a lot of sand or gravel in it, but he found a small amount, found a puddle of water, and followed the technique Mrs. Orlando described. The pan yielded only sand and gravel until his fifth try, when he saw a tiny speck of something that didn't look like gravel. He tried to pick up the speck, but lost it.

Muck ran back to the house and talked to Rose. "Guess what I found at Rocky Bottom!"

"What?"

"Gold!"

"Really? What's it look like?"

"I'm not sure, but it doesn't look like gravel. It's there, all right."

Rose smiled. "Perhaps. Don't get your hopes up."

"I don't only hope. I saw it and it's there. I'll get it, and we'll be rich."

Rose tried to change the subject. "That's fine, Dear. Go pump some water and wash up. Poppa'll be in for supper soon."

"You wait, Momma, you'll see. There's gold down there, and I'll prove it to you someday."

"That's fine, Dear. You wash up now."

Muck didn't try to talk about gold at home after that, but he talked again to Mrs. Orlando the next day. "What do gold miners need to know?"

"How to dig?"

"No, I mean what do they study in school?"

"Maybe geology?"

"What's that?"

"It's the study of rocks and other earth formations."

"Would a gold miner study that?"

"Yes, it could help."

"What do geology people need to study to get ready?"

"Probably math and science, Muck. Why are you interested in geology?"

"Don't you remember? You said Rocky Bottom Creek has gold in it."

"I did?"

"Yes, you did. And I found some yesterday after school."

"Really?"

"Yes, a little. But someday I'll find it all, and be rich, after I learn geology."

"That's great, Muck." Mrs. Orlando's tone changed to a teasing one. "I'll expect all one hundreds on your math and science papers from now on." Muck didn't try again to talk about gold to Mrs. Orlando, so he didn't talk about gold to anyone for a while. But he did try to improve his shaky math performance.

Chapter 14
1948 - 1956

Muck's parents added a telephone during his fifth grade year in school, and could ring up Kenzie and Erroll, a few people in Rounder, and if they wanted to call the operator, people anywhere in the US. The telephone didn't matter to Muck, because his parents didn't allow him to touch it.

Muck graduated from Number Five in April of 1951, at age fourteen. He walked to Rounder High School during his freshman year, but a school bus came by the Paterson farm during his sophomore and later years, and he rode on it. He didn't object when people referred to him as Muck when he entered high school, and indeed called himself that. Skip Barnes also attended RHS; they laughed about the name, even though Skip continued to act offended by him. The tag stuck with him through high school, and even his parents occasionally called him Muck, although his grandparents never did.

His freshman classes at RHS included Science I taught by Mr. Ollie Tollivar. Muck stayed after class one morning during his second week at RHS, to put out a feeler to Mr. Tollivar. "Do you think Jake County could have valuable minerals under it?"

"Valuable minerals? Which ones?"

"Maybe gold?"

"No one's found any as far as I know. Do you know more than I do?"

"Probably not. The Rounder Public Library subscribes to *Prospecting and Mining Journal*, and I look at that sometimes."

"Have you learned anything about Jake County or about Missouri?"

"No, I wondered if you think gold's possible here."

"Of course I think it's possible. Anything is. There's a lot we haven't found, most likely because nobody's looked."

"Great. I gotta go to English class now, but can I talk to you about some plans sometime?"

"Sure, I'll look forward to it. Can you stay a few minutes after school today?"

Muck went to his English and later classes, but didn't focus. He ran up the stairs and down the hall to Mr. Tollivar's empty room when he finished with his last subject. He looked around and found a teachers' meeting in progress in the school library. He saw Mr. Tollivar in the meeting, and waited by the door several minutes, but Principal Henson talked the entire time, and gave no hint of an end. Muck walked home, but the next day he approached Mr. Tollivar at the beginning of science class. "I tried to find you after school yesterday, and didn't find you here, but saw you in a teachers' meeting."

Mr. Tollivar looked away from Muck. "Yes, I know. I saw you out in the hall. I knew about the meeting when we talked, but it slipped my mind. I'll be here this afternoon if you can visit again."

"Sure, I'll be here."

Mr. Tollivar stood in the front of his room with two students when Muck returned at the end of the school day. Muck waited for the students to leave, but they went to a lab bench to work on something instead. He went in the room, glanced at the students, and reminded, "Do you remember what we talked about after class yesterday?"

"Sure do." Mr. Tollivar stopped and waited after those two words.

"Do you have any ideas what I should study in college to learn about it?"

"Geology. I took an introductory course at ALU and they have a strong department there."

"Thanks. I might do that." Muck looked at the two students again and left the room.

Muck walked by Mr. Tollivar's room before and after school several days in a row, and always saw other people. The first time he found Mr. Tollivar alone, he ran into the room. "Have you thought any more about gold in Jake County?"

"Gold in Jake County?"

"Yes, I need to go now." Muck didn't bother Mr. Tollivar further about gold, but later in the year accidentally learned his young math teacher, Miss Crewes, grew up in California. He surmised she might know about gold.

He went through a conversation with her like his earlier one with Mr. Tollivar. After he explained, Miss Crewes asked, "What exactly do you want to do?"

"Rocky Bottom Creek cuts across the south side of my grandparents' farm. The part of the creek east of the road has an almost solid rock bottom, with a bluff just to the north. There's gold under the rock, and probably inside the bluff too. I plan to bust up the rock and drill back into the bluff after I finish at ALU."

"That sounds great, Muck, except the bluff and creek bottom are different—if you find gold in one place, that doesn't guarantee it'll be in the other. Gold in the creek likely came down from upstream, but gold under the bluff probably isn't associated with gold in the creek."

"Do you think my plan is stupid?"

"Absolutely not! You never know what you might find until you look. I've not heard about gold in Jake County, but that only means no one's found it yet. I think it'll be great if you look."

"How much do you think could be there?"

"Any amount, Muck, from none to truck loads."

"Wow! I can hardly wait to graduate from ALU. I'll find it all and be rich."

Miss Crewes laughed. "You'd better hold your horses. You're still a freshman here, so it'll be awhile before you finish at ALU."

"Do you think I should skip ALU?"

"Absolutely not. You'll come out of ALU knowing much more than you know now. If you don't go, and if you realize what you missed, you'll kick yourself black and blue."

"Do you think I should look for gold during summers while I'm in high school?"

"Whether you do is up to you and your parents, but I recommend you wait until you finish at ALU. If you find a little during a summer, you might lose some of it because you don't know how to get it all. Perhaps it's better to wait until you know as much as you can."

"Yeah, you're probably right. And I know my mom thinks it's stupid, so she might not support it."

"Good thinking. Keep me posted. I expect to still be here when you finish at ALU."

"I'll for sure do it. You're the first person I talked to who didn't act like the whole idea is dumb. I know it isn't, and I'm glad you don't think it is. I'll keep you posted—count on it."

Both Paterson families added indoor plumbing and propane heat in 1952 during the summer before Muck's sophomore year, although they didn't add a bathroom to the east house, because it had no suitable space. With those additions, except for the bathroom, they had every home convenience people in Rounder had. Erroll gave up gardening that summer, because he didn't feel well, and Kenzie lacked energy too. Muck took over most of the gardening, became backup milker, and helped Laren with much of the other work Erroll once helped do. Rose took complete meals across the road occasionally, and more often after Muck started his sophomore year at RHS. Both Erroll and Kenzie weakened faster during the last part of the year. Baird and his family—Maye and two children by then, Joseph and Elizabeth—lived in Boston, where Baird worked as Assistant Professor of Mechanical Engineering at a prestigious university. They drove all the way to Rounder at Christmas time, as they always did, but when they left to return to Boston, Erroll went to bed and didn't get up again.

Erroll died Tuesday, February 3, 1953. Muck stayed out of school Wednesday through Friday, and attended the funeral on Friday. Kenzie went on a few weeks and showed little outward sign of loss, but Rose opened a floodgate when she commented, "You're holding up remarkably well, Momma. How do you do it?"

"Oh, Rose. You can't imagine how hard it is. I'm lost without Erroll. I had no idea I depended on him for so much—partly for what he did, but mostly for keeping me in the real world. Sometimes I feel like I'll go crazy without Erroll to joke with me, and tell me I'm silly when I'm afraid. Value your time with Laren, because it will end before you're ready. You and Laren together are such a treasure. I think I'd already be madder'n a hatter without your support."

"You know we support you Momma. Just tell us if there's more we can do."

"I don't want to impose, Rose. You kids are better than I deserve. I know I lean on you, but at the same time, I don't want to be a burden." Kenzie sank rapidly, and she too died, July 12 of the same year. Baird, Maye, Joseph, and Elizabeth were back for both funerals, and all except four-year-old Elizabeth spoke solemnly about finality and loss.

Muck worked as 'second man' on the farm during his last three years of high school. He started as a geology major at ALU in the fall of 1955, but because he came home to help with hay and summer farm work all through his college years, Laren didn't cut back on the farm operation. The Viet Nam war started in 1955, but Muck lacked enthusiasm for the war, and claimed an agriculture and a college exemption. Maybe one of those worked, because his draft board didn't call.

McLaren didn't have a geology class during his first semester at ALU, but wrote about gold as an English assignment. Mr. Rellerburg, his young graduate student English teacher, assigned a writing exercise early in the year that McLaren saw as a get-acquainted opportunity. Students could write 1,500 words about any subject they chose, so McLaren wrote about gold at Rocky Bottom Creek, his plan to find it, and his intention to be rich. When Mr. Rellerburg handed the papers back to the authors with grades on them, McLaren received a C as did most students, but Mr. Rellerburg wrote a short comment on his paper. The comment explained, 'Your writing style and writing performance merit B. Your reasons for thinking you'll find gold merit D. D and B average to C. If you want to succeed in college and in life, forget about gold.' McLaren didn't mention gold to Mr. Rellerburg again, verbally or in writing.

McLaren enrolled in a beginning geology class his second semester at ALU, but after his experience in English class, thought he shouldn't mention gold, not even in a geology class. Dr. Henry, a perfunctory and impersonal teacher, conducted the introductory class; he didn't try to talk to Professor Henry.

McLaren took another geology course during the first semester of his second year, taught by Professor Glaxor. Dr. Glaxor wanted to know every one of his students; he listened and responded when students talked to him.

McLaren stayed after geology class one day, and delayed a moment to avoid breaking into Professor Glaxor's after-class routine. Dr. Glaxor made the first move. "Hello, young man. You look like you have something on your mind."

"Yes, Sir. I want to ask you about gold in Jake County."

"I'm not familiar with gold in Jake County. Where is it?"

"I grew up on a farm about two miles south of Rounder. Rocky Bottom Creek runs across the farm, and I'm pretty sure I can find gold under the rocks."

"Why are you pretty sure?"

"I panned in gravel beside the rocks and found some. Anyway, I want to ask you if you know about any other gold around there."

"Actually, I don't. Anything's possible however."

McLaren smiled. "Yeah, I've heard that before. I wonder if you know for sure about gold in the county."

"No, I don't. Are you a geology major?"

"Yes."

'Then you'll take a class called 'Finding Placer, Lode, and Petroleum Deposits' when you're a senior, and you'll learn there how to evaluate various terrains. Geologists believe most gold deposits in the U.S. are already removed, but their belief doesn't make anything either true or false, of course. Nevertheless, you probably shouldn't build your hopes too high."

"I know it's there, and I intend to find it and be rich. If you think of anything I should know, will you tell me?"

"Of course, and good luck to you."

Rose and Laren came for McLaren when the Christmas break began, and Baird and his family arrived home a day earlier. McLaren invited Baird to walk down to Rocky Bottom with him, and told Baird for the umpteenth time what he planned to do there. Baird adopted a serious manner and suggested, "Let's sit awhile on that log over there." After they sat, he asked, "You're still fixed on gold?"

"Oh, sure. I intend to earn a geology degree at ALU and come back here to dig it out. If I have to make it my life's work, I'll do it. I know it's here."

"Let's suppose it's here and you find tons of it. What then?"

"What do you mean?"

"If you find it, what will you do with it?"

"Sell it and be rich."

"Who will be helped, Muck?"

"Call me McLaren now, Baird, not Muck. But I'll be helped. Who doesn't want to be rich?"

"Do you think there's more than one way to be rich?"

"You mean money rich and some other kind of rich? Maybe, but what good is it to be rich if you don't have money?"

"What about Momma and Poppa? They're not money rich. Are they rich in other ways?"

"Of course."

"What other ways, McLaren?"

"Well . . . they have us."

Baird joked, "*We* might say we make them rich, but an impartial observer might giggle about that. Are they rich in any other ways?"

"They're happy. They do important stuff around here."

"I agree on both counts, McLaren, and I can suggest an 'important stuff' detail. They produce food. Everyone needs food, so that means everyone needs Momma and Poppa, and they know it. Food is like gold, but in another form, a form everybody needs. They're rich because they produce food—something people need—whether they have money or not. Does that seem right to you?"

"Yeah, sure it does. But they'd be more rich if they had money too."

"What could they do with money to make them more happy than they are now?"

"Maybe . . . nothing? They seem . . . adequately happy now."

"Sure they do. But is producing gold comparable in any way to producing food? Will it make everybody need you?"

McLaren stared at the sky for several seconds, then, "I see what you mean Baird. But you don't produce food."

"No, but I produce something people need. Gold is another matter entirely. I can't see how people need you to produce something to make you money rich, but most of them will never use."

"Thanks, Baird. My life's work is to get the gold out of here, and I don't expect to change. But I'll think about what you say. I'll write to you in January and tell you what I decide."

"Fair enough." Baird stood up from the log. "Let's go back to the house."

Chapter 15
1957 - 1959

McLaren and Baird returned to the house, and found Laren and Rose playing with Joseph and Elizabeth, and talking with Maye. Laren welcomed them. "We're glad you're back. We debated awhile ago whether to move across the road into your grandparents' house. What do you think, Baird?"

"It probably needs work doesn't it? I suppose it's been vacant since   " Baird's voice tailed off and died away.

Laren broke Baird's awkward silence. "Yes, it's been empty since your grandparents died. That's three or four years."

"Won't it be easier to stay here?"

McLaren suggested, "Maybe you can rent it. You still have to fix it up, but I can do that next summer and fit it around hay work or whatever else you have for me. I agree with Baird it'll be easier to stay here, but the house over there will literally fall down if you don't keep after it."

Rose nodded. "You boys say exactly what I told Laren. I don't want to move, and there's no reason the two of us need a bigger house. I hope Poppa will listen to you."

Laren refused to argue. "Rose and I'll figure it out, but we can do it later when you're not here to visit."

Baird and his family departed for Boston three days before New Year's, and Rose and Laren took McClaren back to ALU one day after. They informed him on the way they decided to stay in their house and accept his offer to fix up the other house in the summer.

McLaren changed his major to horticulture when he returned to ALU, and didn't mention gold again for a long time, except to explain to Baird, his parents, and Miss Crewes at RHS. He graduated from ALU with a degree in agriculture in the spring of 1959. Baird didn't attend the graduation ceremony, but Rose and Laren did. Rose talked steadily as she helped McLaren with his cap and gown. "Poppa and I are proud of you, Son. Poppa's only forty-one years old, but sometime in the next ten years he'll slow down, and he'll need you. We would never interfere in your life, but we're mighty pleased you changed your major. In geology, you'd probably go some place far away, like Texas or Saudi Arabia, and we'd never see you; we're so proud, and we can't wait to have you home full time again."

After the commencement ceremony ended, McLaren rode back to the farm with Rose and Laren, and talked about how he thought his future life might go as they traveled, and about his life's work. "Baird convinced me to give up my first goal, to find gold in Rocky Bottom Creek, so I drifted without a goal for a while. But now, I intend to make our table gardens at home the most productive in the state, and to add flowers to make them also the most beautiful in the state. I expect to follow in your footsteps and live out my life in a quiet and productive way, right there in Jake County."

Rose replied, "I don't like the sound of 'live out my life'. You sound like you have it planned to the end, but you can't plan that far. Nobody knows what's in their future, not even as far ahead as tomorrow, and you don't either, McLaren."

"I don't mean it that way, Momma. But what can happen to a farmer? Did anything ever happen to you and Poppa?"

"You happened to us, Son. What can be more exciting than that?"

"People have children every day, all around the world. I mean, what new or different thing can happen to a farmer?"

Rose didn't answer, and when they returned to the farm in the afternoon, Laren changed to work clothes and sighed. "I need to go out and do the evening chores."

McLaren inquired, "You need any help?"

Laren looked across the road and answered, "You know the renters we had after you fixed the west house over there? They moved out in the night a couple o' weeks ago. Maybe you can chore with me in the morning to see what I do, but it might be better now to go see if the house needs more repair."

"Whatever you think, Poppa."

McLaren went to look at the house. He saw a broken east window while still in the road, and saw another on the south when he approached the kitchen door. He opened the door and stepped inside, but heard a woman's voice, so he backed out and knocked on the door. The sound stopped when he knocked, so he waited a few seconds and went back in. He checked all the rooms but found nobody, until he opened the front bedroom closet door, and found a woman with blood on her face and her hand over a little boy's mouth. He demanded, "Who are you?"

The woman didn't answer, but tried to run past him. McLaren blocked her exit from the closet and asked again, "Who are you?" The woman still didn't answer so he threatened, "I'll stand here until you tell me."

The woman responded, after a several second delay. "My husband and son and I lived here but we fell behind in the rent, so my husband decided to leave. He said I mustn't know where he went, if I found out I mustn't talk, and he'd show me what he'd do I did talk. He hit me with a kitchen chair and left. Timmy and I remain here, and I truly don't know where my husband is."

"I live across the road and we need to talk with my parents. Come on." McLaren grabbed the woman's arm with one hand and the boy's with the other. He took them across the road and into the house with Rose.

"Is Poppa still in the house?"

"No, who's that?"

"Somebody I found in the other house." McLaren pointed west. "I think we need to call the sheriff."

The woman tried to run when he mentioned the sheriff, but McLaren blocked the door. The woman screamed, "He'll kill me, and Timmy too, if you call the sheriff. Don't you understand?"

Rose assured the woman, "My husband will be in after while, and McLaren's here. Nobody's going to let anybody kill anybody. You're safe here. Can I get you something to eat?"

"Oh would you? And for Timmy? We haven't eaten since the re-frigerator went empty. And can we have a drink?"

Rose put two plates on the table, went to the refrigerator and found, as she put it, 'enough food for a threshing crew.' She put the food on the table, added forks and knives, and drew two glasses of water. Neither the woman nor the boy said thank you, or anything else. They merely ate, fast and long. Rose found butter and a pitcher of milk in the refrigerator and put those on the table too, along with a half loaf of bread. The woman and her son drank the milk and ate the bread. They left nothing except some butter. Rose and McLaren talked to each other while they waited for the woman and the boy to eat. Rose cautioned, "We can't put these people out on the road, because we can see they're in some kind of trouble. I wish Laren would come in."

"He'll be in soon, Momma." He lowered his voice. "But I still think we need to involve the sheriff."

"Do we dare let them stay here?"

"That might be for Poppa to say. But if we all go to sleep, I don't expect them to be here in the morning. A lot of your stuff might go with them when they leave."

"Maybe you should go out and look for Poppa."

"No, I can't do that. She could escape if I'm not here, so we have to wait. I only looked in one closet; I wonder if there're any more over there?"

"We'll have to ask when she finishes eating."

"Do you think she'll tell us the truth, Momma?"

"I don't know. I'm glad you found her and not me. I'd be terrified."

"What do you think I am? Before we go to sleep tonight, I need to go back over there and look in every closet, in the barn, chicken house, and everywhere. We don't know how many of them there are."

"I'll believe any reasonable thing she says McLaren."

"I won't. The husband she accused might be there too. He might be over there with a gun, for all we know."

"I'm not that suspicious, but I wish Poppa'd hurry and get back in—Did you get enough Ma'am? I can probably find more food around here if you want it."

The woman avoided eye contact. "Thank you, but that's enough. Timmy and I needed food and water as much as we now need protection."

Rose frowned. "Can you tell us what you need to be protected from?"

"My husband."

"Where is he?"

"He won't tell me."

Rose continued to frown. "Can he still be in the house over there?"

"No. That's the one place I know he's not—Shh. Somebody's at the door. It's probably him." She looked directly at McLaren. "Don't let him get me. Where can I hide?"

Rose assured, "It's my husband. Open the door, McLaren, he probably has buckets in his hands." McLaren opened the door and started to explain before Laren entered.

Words spilled out from Rose as soon as McLaren finished. "I'm so glad you're back Laren. We need to decide what to do with this woman. She's horribly abused, and it'll be dark in a couple hours."

Laren frowned. "McLaren says she told him she's our renter, so we know she lies. Have you telephoned the sheriff?"

The woman screamed her objection to the sheriff again. Laren looked at Rose. "Can you calm her down? We must call the sheriff. He can still get here before dark if we catch him in his office."

Rose tried to calm the woman, but McLaren had to block the door again. Laren went to the telephone, and the woman screamed and tried again to get out the door when he asked for the sheriff. McLaren maintained his position in front of the door, and the sheriff arrived in his car after only about an hour. McLaren had to physically move the woman away from the door to allow the sheriff to come in. Laren looked like a pint-sized kid beside the sheriff, and the pistol at his side added to his all-business demeanor. He identified himself as Sheriff Lance Erskine of Jake County.

The sheriff looked around and instructed Rose to introduce everybody and explain the problem. "I'm Rose Paterson, and these," she pointed, "are my husband and son. This," she pointed again, "is somebody my son found in the house across the road. I don't know her name."

The sheriff turned to the woman and demanded her name. The woman continued to scream, "He'll kill me!"

"Ma'am, I'm the sheriff and you have to answer my questions. Who's 'he' and how can he kill you with all of us here?"

"He'll kill me! Don't you understand? He'll kill me!"

"Who is he, Ma'am?"

"My husband. He'll kill me."

"Calm down, Ma'am. Is he nearby now?"

"He's over there." The woman pointed west.

"In the house over there?"

"I know he sees your car. He'll kill me."

The sheriff turned to Laren. "We won't get much out of her. You stay with her, and I'll go search the house." He went out, walked across the road, and entered the west house. He came out of the house after a few minutes, and went first into the chicken house, then the laundry house, and finally the barn. He came out of the barn after several minutes, pushing a man in handcuffs in front of him.

Laren reported, "He's got somebody. Found'im in the barn."

The woman intensified her screams. "He'll kill me. If you won't hide me, hide Timmy."

Laren tried to calm her, then Rose tried, and ultimately, McLaren tried. Every effort agitated her more. The sheriff pushed the handcuffed man through the door and inside. The woman suddenly hushed and sat in a chair when she saw him. The man glanced at her and quietly asserted, "I'll kill you, you know."

The woman responded to the man's threat with renewed screams, but the sheriff responded differently. "You trespassed, which is a misdemeanor at most, but now you threatened this woman. You're probably just drunk, but I gotta take you back to Jakesville and hold you in a cell until morning. I hope that'll do it, but if not, I'll keep you there until you can afford a lawyer to get you out." The sheriff turned to the woman and shouted over her screams, "I can take you and the boy back too, and let you sleep in another cell where you'll be safe, if you want me to do it."

Rose suggested the woman and boy stay in her house until morning. Both Laren and the woman protested. Laren warned, "We don't know this woman's character. We don't want her here in the night, and what will we do with her in the morning?"

The woman screamed again, "He'll kill me. He'll kill us all."

A look of extreme impatience or disgust swept over the sheriff's face. "Lady, this man won't kill anybody. I won't let him."

"You can't stop him. You don't know him like I do. You can't stop him."

The sheriff retorted, "Don't tell me I can't. I know where he is, and where he'll be all night, so I sure as shootin' can stop him, and don't tell me I can't."

The woman insisted, "He'll wait years if he has to, but he'll kill me. Then he'll kill Timmy. You can't stop him."

The sheriff ignored the woman from that moment, but turned to Rose. "Ma'am, if you can keep her here overnight, I'll be obliged to you. But I do recommend one of you men," he gestured toward Laren and McLaren, "stay awake all night to make sure she doesn't do something stupid."

Laren asked again, "What will we do with her in the morning?"

"If she screams like this all night, you'll probably shoot'er before morning." He paused. "I don't mean that. You can't shoot'er, but if she's still hysterical at eight o'clock, call me and I'll come back. Maybe I'll figure out a way to handle'er by then."

Laren asked the woman, "Will you consent to stay the night with us?"

The woman screamed again, "He'll kill me. He'll be here in the morning and he'll kill me."

Laren inquired, "Do you prefer to go some other place?"

The woman quieted slightly and then answered, "No."

"Then you'll stay here?"

"Yes."

Laren addressed McLaren. "I'm glad you're here, Son. I don't know how we'd handle this without you. Let's bed these two down in the living room. I'll sit all night on the bottom stair step so she can't get at Rose. You sit all night by the door so she can't get away. All right?"

"All right, Poppa. I wonder if one of us and Momma should go with them, maybe one at a time, to the outhouse before we bed them down?"

"Yeah, sure . . . Sheriff, do we let her go tomorrow?"

"That's a tough question, Mr. Paterson . . . if she's willing, yes, but if she's not willing, call me and I'll come out here and make her go."

McLaren asked Rose, "Can you make a pallet on the floor in the living room?"

"I sure can. I can help you take the woman to the outhouse whenever you're ready, too. Perhaps you can just take the boy around behind the house somewhere. I guess we have everything under control here sheriff, if you want to take what's' is name back to Jakesville."

The sheriff and the guy in handcuffs left. Rose made the pallet, the new people went outside and came back, and everybody except Laren and McLaren went to bed. The woman and her son slept all night; Laren and McLaren fought sleepiness, but stayed awake. Rose invited the new people to join the Patersons for breakfast, and they did. Rose asked the woman after breakfast, "What do you want to do now?"

The woman answered quietly this time, "It doesn't really matter what I do. He'll kill me."

Laren suggested to Rose, "Let's talk. Let her listen if she wants to."

Rose talked first. "We can't push her out, maybe to her death."

Laren responded, "Maybe not, but McLaren and I can't stay in the house around the clock for even a day."

McLaren commented, "It's a dilemma all right. Can we take her any-place where she'll be safe?"

"That's one question, Son, but we can ask another. Is there a place where she'll be safe, and where people around her will be safe? We can't take her anywhere unless we can say yes to both questions. Do you know where that could be Rose?"

"I don't, but I don't think the sheriff does either. I don't want to dump her off on him, because he'll push her out on the street. I wonder if Pastor Thomas can propose anything?"

"I doubt he can, but he might be worth a try. You agree, McLaren?"

"Yeah. Can you ring him up Momma?"

"Yes, but can you men stay in the house until eight o'clock? I shouldn't call into town earlier than that."

The men agreed, Rose called at eight, Pastor Thomas said he'd be right out, and he arrived at 8:05.

"Come on in Pastor, and meet——," Rose threw up her hands, "You never did tell us your name, Ma'am."

The woman answered, "If anybody knows my name they might

lead him to me, and he'll kill me sooner. Just call me Jane. I appreciate you coming out, Pastor, but you can't stop him. He'll kill me."

Pastor Thomas countered, "He won't kill you. I'm Pastor Thomas Ray of Rounder Church and can offer you a Sunday School room at the church today and tonight, and then we can find a safe place for you to go, a place with lots of men around. I'm thinking of a conference room at the furniture factory in Rounder. I'll make the arrangements and you can stay until you're ready to go. Will you come with me?"

The woman went. Laren breathed a sigh and murmured, "That's a relief. I thought we'd never be rid of her."

Rose replied, "We shouldn't think of it as being rid of her. She's in trouble, and she can't stay at the furniture factory forever. She needs to be protected and she probably needs to work. We can't merely wash our hands and say she's gone."

"Why not, Rose? We put ourselves out for her already. What more can we do?"

"Momma's right, Poppa. Pastor Thomas'll help her for a day or two, but we need to work with him to find something more permanent for Jane, or whatever her name is."

"We have all day to talk about it, but we're already late with our chores. Come on and watch me this morning, then maybe you can take over some of it in a few days. We probably should both go back over to the house and look all through it today, and maybe walk all over the farm. We know Jane lies; she might be hiding something else over there. Rose, put a chair in front of the door as soon as we leave, and don't move it for anybody except us."

Laren and McLaren went to do chores, and Rose stayed alone in the house until they came in with milk. McLaren announced, "We're off to look around on the west side of the road now, but we'll be back for lunch."

"You two be careful. I don't want to lose either of you."

"Right, Momma. That's why we decided to go together. We'll be careful."

The men found nothing on the other farm, but Rose continued to talk about the evening before. "I tried to get my mind off last night's 'guest' while you were gone, but couldn't do it. Do either of you know how we can help that poor woman?"

"Forget it, Rose. She lied to us once, and she's probably still doing it." Laren paused when the telephone rang two longs and a short, and then pointed at it. "That's us, Rose."

Rose answered the telephone, talked briefly, and returned to the conversation. "That was Sheriff Erskine on the telephone. He says the man he hauled out of here last night is Roy Simms, wanted for murder in Illinois, for bank robbery in Illinois and Missouri, and he'll be in jail a long time. The sheriff says our 'Jane' is really Celeste Simms, his wife, and he's checking to see if she knows about any of Roy's crimes. He says he'll have to arrest her if she does."

Chapter 16
1959

"Maybe she knows about Roy's crimes Momma. Maybe that's why she thinks the man'll kill her."

"She's wrong about the guy killing her, because the sheriff says he's going to be extradited to Illinois to face the murder charge. He says it's an open and shut case, and if the guy ever gets out, it will only be for enough time to come to a Missouri court to face bank robbery charges. He figures the guy'll get a life sentence for the murder."

"Maybe it will ease Jane's—Celeste's, or whatever—mind if she knows that, Momma."

"You're right, McLaren. I'll ring up Pastor Thomas and ask him to tell her."

"No, Momma, I'll take the car in to Rounder and tell her myself. Shall I tell her she might be a suspect too?"

"No, let Sheriff Erskine tell her if he finds anything. Why bother her about it if he doesn't?"

"I'd want to know if it was me, Momma."

Rose frowned. "If you tell her, you might set her off again. Do you want to do that?"

"No, not that. I won't tell her."

McLaren went to Rounder Church after lunch and talked first with Pastor Thomas, then with Celeste and Timmy. When McLaren came home, Rose told him Laren went out after lunch also, so only he and Rose talked. McLaren reported Pastor Thomas persuaded furniture factory management to take Celeste in for a few days, and she said she'd feel safe there surrounded by three shifts of men.

Rose responded, "We need to learn if she needs a job, and if she'll eventually feel safe outside the factory. From what the sheriff says, I think she will be, but it doesn't matter if she doesn't believe it."

When Rose and McLaren finished, Rose went back to Rounder Church, and asked Pastor Thomas about a job for Celeste. The pastor answered, "I'm way ahead of you on that one, Rose. The furniture factory wants a secretary, and Celeste says she's experienced and qualified. I hope the factory will hire her to work right there. Timmy can stay in the church daycare until school starts, so all she'll need is a more permanent place to live. I have a couple inquiries out on that now."

Rose thanked Pastor Thomas and went home to tell Laren and McLaren. She found neither in the house, but saw McLaren across the road. Rose went over to tell him about her visit with Pastor Thomas, and McLaren commented, "Maybe the situation'll turn out all right. On another topic, this house looks a mess but the problems are cosmetic. I can fix it in a week or so, but then what will you do with it?"

"Let's talk to your Poppa about that question before you waste time here. Have you seen him?"

"No, I don't know where he is, but he'll be back here for supper, you can bet on that, Momma."

Rose and Laren asked McLaren to fix the house and then sleep in it, merely to keep it up, but to have meals with them. They also asked him to take over the gardens and orchards on both farms because of his horticulture knowledge, but they told him they needed him to help with chores and other farm work as well.

McLaren responded, "Yes, I'll enjoy using what I know, and we can get back to normal around here when the house is fixed and Celeste is straightened out."

Rose grinned. "Do you expect to recognize normal if you see it?"

He answered with a laugh instead of with words.

McLaren repaired the west house, moved into it, and hoed weeds from the various gardens. He returned to an earlier conversation with

Rose one day during lunch. "You asked me a few weeks ago if I expect to recognize normal. It's here, and I recognize it."

"Ha."

McLaren turned to Laren. "I think I'll wait to plan garden improvements until winter, but I have a question for you now. Why don't you buy a used baler so you can put baled hay instead of loose hay in the barns?"

"I respect what they taught you in college, McLaren, but I've learned right here we can't spend money unless we really need something. If we only want it, that's not a good reason."

"I agree with you, Poppa. But almost all the other farmers around here have a baler, and they hire Rounder High School boys to haul in the hay. You can't find people to trade hay work with anymore. Because your crew is nobody but us, we're slow, we don't get all the hay cut at the right time, and some of it always gets wet. A baler'll save you more money than it'll cost. You already have the tractor, and it'll make you more if you find more ways to use it."

"That's where you're wrong, McLaren. After we buy a baler, we'll have to buy a different rake, we'll have to buy an elevator—we have a good hayfork already—and we'll have to pay the RHS boys. The baler won't be the end of it, and there may never be an end."

"You're right about paying the boys Poppa, but except for them, you can do it all yourself, and faster than before. You won't have to work weeks on it, then work more weeks paying back neighbors' help, even if you could find the help. You can stand up to all that work now, but the day'll come when it'll be too much for you."

"Yeah, that day'll come, but that's why you're here, McLaren."

"Poppa! Is that the only reason I'm here?"

"Well, no, I don't mean it that way. I'll think about it, but I don't want to rush into it this year. I always make mistakes when I rush into things. I don't say I'll agree to it next year; just that I'll think about it."

Laren mowed hay the last week in May, and continued with hay through June. One June morning when McLaren pitchforked hay in the east barn loft, soaking wet with sweat, Rose ran out of the house to yell at him. "McLaren. McLaren. You have a telephone call in the house."

McLaren came down the loft ladder and ran to the house. "Hello."

"I'm Art Neal, Chief Groundskeeper at Central Surgical in Kansas City. I want you to come and take over our flowers and turf. I can offer you $490 a month."

"How'd you find me? I haven't looked for a job."

"I know you haven't. Professor Bumgarner at ALU gave me your name. He says you're top notch, and I want you on our team."

"How soon do you need an answer?"

"I need it now."

"Then I'm afraid I have to say no, Mr. Neal. I need to think about it for a while before I can say yes to you or no to my parents."

"Don't say no. I'll give you a couple days. This is Friday; can I call you back Monday at nine am?"

"Can you make it seven? I'm busy here, and don't want to wait around until nine for a telephone call."

"Sure, I'll call you at seven o'clock Monday."

"Thanks. Bye."

Rose listened to McLaren's side of the conversation and asked, "What was that about?"

"Somebody offered me a job. I need to think about it over the weekend."

"You don't plan to take it do you?"

"I need to get back in the barn. Poppa's waiting for me. We can talk at lunch."

McLaren went back to the barn and resumed his work. He waited to explain until he and Laren went to the house for lunch. "A guy in

Kansas City offered me a job. He'll call back Monday morning to see if I'll take it."

"What will you do if you take it?"

"Be in charge of grass and flowers, Poppa."

"How much does it pay?"

"$490 a month, Poppa."

"McLaren! That's more than your Poppa and I made our entire first year on the farm!"

"Yes, Momma, it's a lot, and it'll mean you won't have to split farm income with me."

"I hope you know, McLaren, Poppa and I don't ever want to influence you on a job decision, but splitting income isn't something we worry about. Most of what we have here isn't in money form anyway, and when it comes to food and our labor, we give away more than we keep, so don't let that part factor in."

"Looking after flowers and grass might be easier than working with you, Poppa!"

"That's what I'm afraid of, Son. Whichever way you go, know we'll appreciate your help here, or will wish you well somewhere else."

"You know what, Poppa? I talked with Baird years ago about money, and we concluded it's not what it's cracked up to be. I'll turn the guy down when he calls."

"Oh, McLaren, please do say no to him. You'll make your Poppa and me so happy."

Laren looked sideways at Rose, and then spoke to McLaren. "I hope you stay here, but you should think about it before you decide."

"I've decided, Poppa. I'd rather dodge hay you send over my head than tend flowers in Kansas City. I'll stay. I might not even wait in the house on Monday for the call. Will you deliver the message, Momma?"

"If that's what you want me to do, I'll do it with glee."

"Good. We settled it then. Do either of you expect to need the car this evening?"

"We've not needed the car during an evening for years." Laren smiled as he said it. "Where you headed?"

"There's a discussion group for young singles at Rounder Church tonight."

Rose and Laren grinned at each other, then Laren and McLaren finished their lunch and went back out to put more hay in the barn.

McLaren stopped at Rounder Service to gas the car on the way to the church. Skip Barnes pumped the gas and commented, "Hey, Muck. You got the fancy degree, but I got the payin' job. Where's the justice in that?" Skip smiled as he said it, but McLaren thought his voice had an edge to it.

"Justice is what you make of it, I guess." McLaren grinned, paid, and continued to the church.

McLaren participated in the discussion at the church, then tried and failed to get to the exit before a group of three young ladies caught him. One of them professed an interest in the preceding discussion. "Hello. I'm Michelle. You're McLaren, I think?" McLaren nodded. "I'm terribly interested in a comment you made about the value of money. I suspect your lack of interest in it means you're absolutely loaded with it. Is that true, McLaren?"

"Perhaps it depends on how you define loaded. You loaded?"

Michelle giggled. "Maybe I could repeat your answer." Michelle looked her two friends away and continued. "I hear you have a college degree. Is that true?"

"Yeah, I suppose so."

"Does that mean you have job offers?"

"If I count my present job, I have two. You have any?"

Michelle giggled again. "I don't see a ring on your finger. Are you single?"

"I showed up at a discussion group for singles didn't I? You single?"

Michelle giggled yet again, but wriggled her naked ring finger at McLaren. "You busy now?"

"Well, actually I'm about to be. I need to sleep a ton tonight."

"How disappointing. You want my phone number?"

"Under different circumstances I might, Michelle, but I want to stay off my telephone so I can receive more job offers." McLaren took another step toward the door.

Michelle moved to step in front of him. "I'll be here Sunday morning. Look for me."

"I might look for you if my Momma lets me come here."

"Oh, McLaren!" Michelle giggled more. "You'll be here. You were here the last three Sundays in a row."

McLaren pushed Michelle aside. "Look, Michelle, I'm not interested in girls like you. I must go."

"Girls like me? What am I like, McLaren? Huh?"

"Oh, Michelle, I'm sorry. You're right, I don't know what you're like. I'm sure you're very nice, but I do have to go."

"Can you squeeze in a few minutes to take me over to Rounder Drive-N-Go for something to drink?"

"Yeah, I guess I owe you that. You ready to go?"

Michelle and McLaren went out in the church parking lot to the car. "This your car McLaren?"

"It's my parents'."

"I bet your car is newer than this one, right?"

"Maybe someday. You want to get in?"

They went to Rounder Drive-N-Go, but sat and talked for a while before they ordered root beer floats. After their root beer floats, they talked more, and had chocolate malts. McLaren took Michelle home late, parked the car in his parents' drive, and made it to bed in the west house a little after one o'clock.

He straggled over to breakfast late on Saturday morning, and his parents ribbed him. Rose started it. "Do you want to know when you came home last night?"

"Do you know?"

"Yes. You actually came home this morning, rather than last night." McLaren failed to see humor, but Rose and Laren laughed.

"It doesn't matter when I got home. I'll carry my end of the load today."

Laren grinned. "Starting with a late breakfast?"

Rose piled on. "Perhaps Poppa will allow you to take an afternoon nap." She grinned too, and Laren grinned even more.

McLaren ate fast, feigned excessive energy when he finished, bounded out the door, and called, "Come on, Poppa. We have a lot of work to do today."

McLaren looked for Michelle when he arrived at church the next day, and saw her sitting with her two friends from Friday night, several rows behind him. He turned and made a discreet wave, but didn't go back to sit with her. Rose looked back too, and asked "Is that her?"

McLaren played dumb. "Is that who?"

"Your girl friend, you know who."

"Yeah, that's her."

"Why don't you go back and sit with her? Poppa sits with me."

"You're different. You're married."

"We didn't get to be married by sitting apart."

"Leave it alone, will you, Momma?"

Rose gave McLaren a respite, but after the service, she urged him to invite Michelle to Sunday dinner; he didn't invite her that Sunday, but he did the next. He made many trips to Rounder to see Michelle, and brought her to the farm for dinner every subsequent Sunday until the third Sunday in August.

Chapter 17
1959 - 1962

The Rounder Parks volunteer board invited McLaren to contribute to their regular second Tuesday meeting on July 14, 1959, when the board planned to consider grounds upgrades. He visited the Parks office on the eighth to learn what the board wanted. When he later attended the meeting, he impressed the board with elaborate plans, drawings on poster board, and detailed technical talk; he came out of the meeting as the new chairman of the Rounder Parks grounds committee. He didn't change the parks much in 1959, but persuaded the committee to vote to grade and terrace a few locations.

Rose invited Celeste and Timmy Simms for lunch on Saturday, August 15, and went to their rooming house to pick them up in the car and bring them out. Laren and McLaren made it a point to finish their week's work by noon, and to show up for a big meal.

Laren inquired about Celeste's husband, Roy. Celeste answered, "He's in jail in Illinois. I think we're free from him. I don't want to be happy he's in jail, but in a way I am, because it's the only way Timmy and I can be safe."

Celeste stopped talking, and McLaren asked about her work. "I'm so happy with my work. I'm the general manager's secretary at the furniture factory; he's a good boss and the salary is decent. Timmy and I live in the rooming house now, so we only eat stuff we don't have to cook, but I think we can rent a regular house in a couple of years if I keep the job."

"I didn't know you can't cook in the rooming house . . . will you come out here for Sunday dinner each week? We'll pick you up at church." Rose hesitated and glanced at McLaren. "McLaren's

Michelle already comes out here on Sundays, and you'll round out the group."

Celeste frowned, looked at Timmy, waited a moment, then delivered a revelation. "Yes, Michelle told us at work she fixed her sights on McLaren. She supposedly works in an office next to mine at the furniture factory, but she's a joke, because she doesn't actually do anything. I think you should watch her, McLaren, because she brags she has you wrapped around her little finger and is about to marry you and get your farm. I don't know how she talks around you, but she'd scare you to death if you could hear her talk at work."

A silent spell followed Celeste's disclosure. Rose and Laren looked from McLaren to Celeste and back again. Laren eventually asked, "What'll you do, Son?"

McLaren responded after a shorter pause. "I have a date with Michelle tonight and I'll ask her about all that. I can deal with Michelle. Don't worry about the farm."

Laren cleared his throat. "You know we don't want to interfere, Son. But we don't want her to get the farm either. Celeste says there's danger there, so be cautious."

"Forget about it, Poppa. I know Michelle and I know what I'm doing."

The group quickly dropped talk about Michelle, and engaged in unrelated conversation during and after the meal, but McLaren didn't say much. Rose renewed her Sunday dinner invitation to Celeste and Timmy, and Celeste accepted.

McLaren and Michelle planned to drive over to Jakesville to see a play that night, but McLaren picked her up and suggested they drive only to the edge of town to a Lake Rounder overlook. "The play'll be a good one in Jakesville, McLaren. I very much want to see it."

"We might still make it. What kind of financial future do you see for yourself?"

"I see a good one. I'll quit my job, and you'll get title to——"

McLaren interrupted, "I see. I hear you and Celeste Simms work together."

"Yes, Celeste is such a bore. Do you know her beyond what she says at your house?"

"Sort of, Michelle. Can you guess what she says about you?"

"Probably a bunch of lies, whatever it is."

"She says you brag at work you'll get our farm. Can that be true?"

Michelle emitted wails and tears, but between sobs, "Even if it is, what does it matter to you? It's not your farm, after all."

"I'm going to take you back home Michelle. Our farm is ours, not yours, and never will be. I belong there and not here. You belong here and not there."

"McLaren, what came over you? You don't believe that Celeste woman instead of me do you?"

"Here's your house, Michelle. Bye."

Michelle opened the car door, and ran out in a huff. He returned to the farm before his parents retired, and told them what happened.

McLaren cruised through the remainder of 1959. He and Laren bought an almost new baler, a used hay elevator with a gasoline engine on it, and a used side-delivery rake at a farm sale in March, 1960. The rake didn't cost much, but needed a few new teeth, and McLaren added them before the end of the month. Laren conceded the baler made the 1960 hay season go fast, and because both he and McLaren worked to haul hay to the barn, they paid two RHS boys for only two days. The cost for boys would have been none at all, except Laren didn't want to risk rain on baled hay.

The flower-bordered gardens at the farm were spectacular that summer, and Rose commented she suspected people from Rounder drove past specifically to look at the gardens. The grounds at Rounder Parks, consisting mainly of trees, grass, and flowers, attracted even more people than the gardens at the farm. The Park Director claimed she saw almost twice as many picnics on Park grounds as the year before, and weddings went from one the year before to three in 1960.

During a Sunday dinner at the farm in November of 1960, Timmy asked two questions. "Now that I'm eight, will you call me Tim instead of Timmy?"

"Of course, Timmy—Tim. From this moment on, you'll be Tim to me—and I bet you'll be Tim to Momma and Poppa." McLaren looked at Rose and Laren.

"Yep. You're Tim now, anytime you're in this house. We always thought you looked more like a Tim than a Timmy." Laren smiled big.

"Thanks Mr. Paterson. McLaren?"

"Yes, Tim?"

"Rounder Parks started a football program for kids this fall, and they have a father-son banquet Saturday night. They say the father part doesn't have to be real. Will you come with me?"

"Tim, my schedule's awful busy, but it happens to have a hole in it on Saturday night and I can't think of anything I'd rather do. What time should I pick you up?"

"They said it starts at five o'clock. It's at the Community Building at Shier Park."

"How about if I show up at the rooming house at 4:30? I'll wait out front."

"Great, McLaren. I can't wait to tell the other guys. Thanks a bushel and a peck."

McLaren bought his gas at Rounder Service for a while, but saw no change in Skip Barnes, so he switched to Jake County Co-op in the fall of 1960, and also persuaded his parents to buy a smaller, cheaper car that fall. They bought a brand new Studebaker Lark.

McLaren dated girls after Michelle during the early 1960's, but none seriously. He put most of his energy into his farm work and gardens. He enlarged the farm gardens and orchards so much he became a regular vendor at Rounder Farmers' Market, and made the farm gardens so beautiful Rose clearly had it right; people did drive out from Rounder to look. Similarly, Rounder Parks attracted even more visitors during 1961 and 1962 than in 1960. Rounder Parks won state and regional awards in 1961, and in January of 1962, the Jake County Commission asked McClaren to upgrade the grounds around the courthouse in Jakesville.

McLaren talked to his parents about whether to accept the courthouse work. "What do you think, Poppa? They'll pay for it—not much, but enough to cover the travel cost. The bigger problem is, I'll be gone from the farm a few more days, and I have conflicting desires. I want to take the job, but don't want to leave you here to do all the work."

Although McLaren asked Laren, Rose answered. "You do it, McLaren. We're both proud of your success. We didn't anticipate you'd go this way when you came back home, but we're proud of you." Laren nodded his agreement.

"OK, I'll do it. I thought I'd set my life direction, but I really have this time. I'll divide my time between the farm and nearby gardens, and watch things get better."

Laren shook his head no. "Hold on there, Son. Don't count your chickens before they hatch. The sky may fall in on you tomorrow. Nobody knows what the future holds."

"Poppa, you're usually right, but there's no way my life can turn out to be anything but boring."

"You bored now, Son?"

"No, Poppa, but it's still all new. After I've done it a few years, it might—I don't want to say boring, maybe I should say I'll have it made."

Laren almost choked, then raised his voice. "Son, Son. Nobody ever has it made. I don't know what's going to happen to you, but you for sure don't want to tempt God by saying what you just said. I want the best for you, but you know little about tomorrow, and nothing about five years from now."

McLaren laughed, and made Laren's frown deepen more. "OK, Poppa. I won't have it made. As Grandpoppa used to say, we have to wait and see."

"Right, Son."

McLaren walked to Shier Park in Rounder on a Saturday morning in early March, 1962. He knelt to study soil conditions in a flowerbed he planned alongside a walking trail, and felt a touch on his shoulder. He jumped up, turned around, turned red, and stammered, "O—Oh—Hi Miss Crewes."

Miss Crewes smiled. "I saw you here and stopped to say how beautiful Rounder parks are now. But you're long gone from RHS and you don't have to call me Miss Crewes anymore. My name is Christine, but my friends call me Chris. Will you call me Chris?"

"Of course. Chris. I told you I dropped my gold effort. Would you like to go over to Rounder Diner for coffee so I can explain why?"

"I'm on my way to—"

"I don't want to keep you from anything important, but you name a time, and I can go. Farm work isn't pressing right now."

"Actually, I can go now if it works for you."

"Great. I'm on foot; can you take me there?"

McLaren and Chris went to the diner, McClaren explained about the gold and went far beyond; they talked more than two hours. McLaren wanted to continue when they eventually walked out to the parking lot. "Chris, you're not like other girls—women—I've dated—I mean I've talked to. You're more grown up, and more settled, if you know what I mean. Can we see each other again, maybe Monday evening after school?"

"McLaren, I'm flattered. I like you too, but I have to tell you something. My dad's gone now, and my mom needs someone to help her with ordinary living. I plan to resign from RHS at the end of the school year and go back to San Francisco to live with her. Although

I'd love to date you, for both our sakes, I don't want us to start something only for me to end it."

"Oh. I'm glad you told me." Both McLaren and Chris were quiet a moment, then McLaren resumed. "Maybe we can see each other without thinking of us as dating. I really don't want to say goodbye to you months before you go. When will you go?"

"I'll go in May, a week after school's out."

"Can we see each other until then?"

"I'll love it McLaren, if we realize it will end soon."

"What are the chances you can persuade your mom to move to Rounder?"

Chris shook her head and smiled. "None at all, McLaren. I'll go before the end of May."

He walked back to the farm and Chris drove away to somewhere in her car. He and Chis went out often until the end of the school year, and tried to not talk about their outings as dates. McLaren suffered a bleak day, however, when he watched Chris drive away from her apartment in Rounder the last time.

He didn't have as much time for Tim as he wanted during March and April, but had a thought when Celeste talked about her move from the rooming house. He stated his idea the day after Chris left Rounder. "Poppa, I like the privacy I have when I sleep across the road, but it seems a waste of a house. You can get rent on it if I move all the way back in with you and Momma."

"You have a renter in mind, Son?"

"Yes, how about Celeste and Tim?"

Laren laughed. "You have a thing for older women, don't you, Son?"

"That's not it at all, Poppa. But Celeste needs a place to live, you can always use more income, and if they live there, I'll be able to do more for Tim."

"So we're talking about three things here. Celeste, the house, and Tim. Which is the big one?"

"All of'em, Poppa. Maybe Tim mostly."

"Or maybe Celeste mostly?"

"Poppa, I swear to you, I want to help Celeste, but I'm not attracted to her. I've never dated her, and never will."

"You know of course, we want to have you full time in our house. I'll talk to Momma about renting the west house."

"Great. Maybe today? Celeste and Tim might find something else if you wait."

"Why do you think Celeste wants to live two miles out of Rounder when she might find something in town?"

"She has a car now. I don't think two miles will matter."

"I'll talk to Momma, and if she agrees, she'll be the one to talk to Celeste about it."

"Great, Poppa."

Celeste and Tim moved to the west house. Rose gave them all the milk, eggs and garden produce they could handle, and Tim became like McLaren's shadow. He followed McLaren all over the farm, and even went with him to check on gardens in Rounder and Jakesville.

It appeared McLaren might be right about his life being settled, all the way through 1962. He won awards and praise for his horticulture work again, including on the courthouse grounds.

Chapter 18
1962 - 1963

Institutions in Kansas City, Springfield, and St. Louis called McLaren about landscaping contracts, even before the end of 1962. The first came on a Wednesday early in December from a large college. He discussed the offer at supper with Rose and Laren. "They want a complete proposal. Not merely recommendations, but estimated timelines, costs to establish, costs to maintain, contingency plans, the expected number of employees they'll need to add, and who knows what else. I can do some of it from here, but I have to go there to hear their ideas, and to measure some things before I come back. And maybe I shouldn't come back until I finish, because it will be easier to find most of the data I need, right on the college campus."

Rose responded, "You know how to do everything they want, and in my opinion you're the best person in the state to do it. Why do you even ask us about it?"

"Well, Momma, it's not that I don't know how to do it. But the job'll take time away from the farm and away from Tim. They offer pay and plenty of it, but I'm not sure it's worth it. I can't take your car away that long, so I'll have to buy one, but worse, I'll have to oversee part of it and won't be here for the hay season. You'll be forty-eight in March, Poppa. I once said I'd stay here and help you with the heavy work, but I can't help when I'm gone. I try to fill in for Tim's dad where I can, but I can't do that either if I'm not here."

"I can handle the farm, Son. I came on board about the baler a little slow, but now we have it, I can do it all except the haul-in part, and decent high school guys helped us last year. I can probably get them

back this year. Don't worry about the farm, and as for Tim, he can follow me around as well as he can you."

"I appreciate what you say and it will help me decide, but I plan
to let it rest until Friday before I tell them yes or no."

McLaren called the college Friday to accept the offer, but re
ceived another for an equally large job across the state on Monday,
plus one more on Tuesday. He struggled again with where his ob-
ligation should be as he chored with Laren on Tuesday afternoon.
"You remember the college job we talked about last Wednesday,
Poppa?"

"Sure, you told'em you'll take it. You're not fixing to change
your mind are you?"

"No, but I have two more offers about like it. If I say yes to them
all, they'll take me almost completely off the farm for the summer."

"If you had nothing else to consider, would you take the jobs?"

"Oh, yes. They're good jobs, every one of 'em."

"Then take'em."

"What about the farm? What about Tim? All the jobs taken together will amount to a full time job. I'll be away from the farm
practically all summer."

"You're good at what you do, Son. People all over the state
know that. You should do as much of it as you can, and leave the
farm to Momma and me. Tim has a momma, and I can help out with
him some. He's not your boy, and you mustn't feel responsible for
him."

"What I 'feel' doesn't matter. I'm partly responsible for the
farm, and for Tim too. I can't just shuck them."

"I admire you for that, Son, but you take it too far. You need to
do what you trained for, what you do uncommonly well. You can
feel a trace of responsibility for as many different things as you
want, but your really big responsibility is to do the best work you
can—whatever it is and wherever you find it."

"Thanks for your perspective Poppa. I'll think about what you say, but I won't accept or reject anything today. I'll try to decide tonight, and call them tomorrow."

"While you think, keep in mind all those people in those cities you'll let down if you say no."

Laren asked McLaren at breakfast the next morning what he decided. "I'll take both jobs, which makes three total, but that's all I can handle. If anybody else calls, Momma, and if they have more job offers, tell'em I already have a full load—I don't even want to talk to them."

McLaren worked away from the farm most of the summer. He received enough pay to buy a 1957 Dodge half-ton pickup, to give his share of farm income back to his parents, to put money in a college fund for Tim, and to have plenty left over. He stayed home during most of November and talked to Rose and Laren about the summer at lunch one day. "I had a whirlwind season, but the college and the others are set up so they can continue on their own now. Perhaps I can do my real work here next year."

Rose responded, "Yes McLaren, you're twenty-six years old now, and it's time for you to settle down, and find a wife. When Poppa was twenty-six, we already had you."

McLaren grinned. "I won't worry about that, and I hope you won't either. But just think about all the beautiful young things I met in all the exotic places I visited last summer." He continued to grin. "I could probably have ten of'em climbing all over me."

Rose grinned too. "No need to take a good thing too far, McLaren."

"I might go to Rounder in a few days and troll the streets, but for now I wanta go back to normal."

Rose grinned again. "I know you won't 'troll the streets,' but it can't hurt to notice the young ladies. It's time for you to find one."

"You don't need to harp at me, Momma. I understand what you mean."

McClaren resisted every womanly advance he encountered for the remainder of 1963. However, he went off to California to speak and consult in January of 1964, and scanned every crowd he saw for Chris. He didn't know for sure he saw her, but saw a woman with a similar smile in San Francisco. After the end of his talk, he tried to move through the crowd and approach her, but she left the auditorium before he could talk to her.

McLaren returned to Rounder by a southern route, through Phoenix, Tucson, El Paso, and Lubbock. He flew on airplanes from place to place, but rented a car at each city. He fulfilled a short consulting contract in each city, and also spoke to at least one group in each place. He came back to Rounder on Wednesday, March 20, with more pay already than the farm would have provided him for the year, so he topped off Tim's college fund, and again took no share of farm income.

McLaren talked to Rose the same day he returned to the farm. "I've been away from Tim too long; I'll be surprised if he remembers me. He's ten years old now, and I think I neglected him too much already."

"You didn't neglect him, McLaren, but he's in a school play this Friday night. He'll be thrilled if you take him and watch the play."

"Great idea, Momma. I'll ask him about it as soon as the school bus comes."

McLaren met Tim at the school bus that evening. "Hey, Tim, I finally came back. I bet you thought I was gone for good."

"I knew you'd come back, McLaren, and I'm glad you did. Can I help you with your chores tonight?"

"Sure, and besides that, I hope we can go together to your school play on Friday."

"Yeah! Yeah! Nothing could be better!"

"Good. What time should I pick you up?"

"How about if you ride with my mom and Aunt Sue. They're gonna go too."

"That'll work. Do you want to come right home with them, or would you rather go over to Rounder Drive-N-Go for ice cream afterward?"

"Aunt Sue says Mom'll take us over there, and she'll treat. You want to go too?"

"Yes, I suppose so. Who's your Aunt Sue?"

"She's my aunt, Mom's little sister."

"Oh, is she a girl?"

"No, she's an old lady. Almost as old as Mom."

"Interesting. Is she staying with you and your mom?"

"Only a few days. She lives in Kansas City, but came out to go to my play."

"What time Friday will you leave?"

"I have to be there early, so we'll leave at 6:10."

"Will you come by for me, or should I meet you at your house?"

"They'll come by for you. I'll make'em do it."

"Great. I'll go down to the west barn now and start chores. Come on out after you change your clothes."

"Yeah. I'll be there in about three minutes."

McLaren washed up and donned clean clothes before 6:10 on Friday evening. He watched for Celeste's car, and when it pulled into the driveway he went out and sat beside Tim in the back seat, because Celeste and Sue occupied the front seats. Tim had a minor part in the play, but performed it well. McLaren, Celeste, and Sue didn't converse much during the play, and they talked mostly to Tim at Drive-N-Go. Celeste parked her car there, Sue bought ice cream, and they ate it in the car. They ate quickly, stayed at the drive-in only a few minutes, and everybody got out of Celeste's car when they returned to the west house. McLaren said he'd walk home, but lingered a moment to talk with Celeste and Sue. He asked Sue, "Do you expect to be at Celeste's long enough for me to show you the farm tomorrow morning?"

Tim started to say something, but Celeste snatched his arm and steered him into the house, leaving only Sue to answer McLaren. "I'm here until Celeste takes me back. I suppose she'll have to do it by Sunday afternoon, because we both work on Monday, but until then I have loads of leeway."

"Great, Sue. How will it be if I'm over here by seven o'clock?"

"I'll be here with bells on, McLaren."

"Tim'll probably want to go along. Is that all right with you?"

"That's what I like about you, McLaren. What I like is that Tim likes you, that is. If Tim likes you, you gotta be all right."

McLaren laughed. "Well, whatever. I better run home, because I'm pretty sure Momma's looking out the window at us."

"We can't have that, can we? I'll see you tomorrow."

McLaren endured an inquisition from Rose at Saturday breakfast. "You stood and talked a long time with Celeste's sister last night, McLaren."

"Come on, Momma, it couldn't have been more than a couple minutes."

"But who counts when they're having fun? What's she like?"

"What's who like?"

"Don't play dumb with me, McLaren. I happen to know you too well, and to know you're not dumb."

"I'm not deliberately dumb. I can answer your question when you tell me who you mean."

"Celeste's sister, McLaren. Sue."

"Oh, Sue. She's all right, I guess."

"All right? Is that all? I bet you plan to see her again, right?"

"Yeah."

"When?"

"In about a half hour."

"See! What did I tell you? She's much more than 'all right,' isn't she?"

"Do you want a ten page written report, Momma? Can't I talk to anyone without the third degree from you?"

"Maybe you're right, McLaren. Finish your breakfast and then go have fun." Rose giggled. "With Sue."

McLaren showed up at Celeste's door about five minutes early, but Sue came out immediately when he knocked. "Where's Tim?"

"Celeste made him stay in the house. He's not happy."

"Well, I think we can talk better alone, but I hate to leave Tim un-happy."

"He might get over it."

McLaren showed Sue parts of the farm he hadn't walked on in years. They walked more than two hours, plus they sat about a half hour on a log by Rocky Bottom Creek. They agreed to go on a true date that eve-ning, to a social at Rounder Church.

McLaren detailed his views about Sue to Rose at lunch. "Momma, you sometimes know more than I give you credit for. Sue truly is more than all right. She's kind of busy, with a job in a library and a volunteer job as a violin player in her church orchestra, but she's free most week-ends. She lives in what she calls a rented antique house on the east side of Kansas City. She likes the farm, and she likes Tim."

Rose did her 'I told you so' smile. "And I suppose she likes you?"

"Maybe."

"If she does, she has good judgment. Everybody with good judgment likes my boy."

McLaren and Sue dated every Friday and Saturday evening except when Sue's orchestra played on a weekend evening, and even then he sat in the audience. Laren joked that McLaren wore out his pickup driving it to Kansas City. He turned down three good-paying garden jobs that spring, plus five opportunities to speak, to stay on the farm and to date Sue. He tried to make up for earlier absences from the farm and neglect of Tim, and thus made Tim and his family happy. He repeated his 'nor-mal and boring' comments to his parents, and they let them pass.

Chapter 19
1963

Sue visited the farm for several days around Christmas in 1963, and split her time between Celeste and Tim, and McLaren. All joined for Christmas day dinner with the three Patersons normally at home, plus Baird, Maye, Joseph and Elizabeth. People packed the east house until mid-afternoon, when Baird and his family left for their long drive back to Boston.

McLaren received a letter from a Pastor Westerson in the UK the day after Christmas. He offered McLaren a large payment for a series of three lectures in Inverness, plus a smaller amount for a day's consultation on landscaping at Tiny Kirk, in his capacities as Chair of the Inverness Cultural Society and as Pastor of Tiny Kirk. The lectures would be on Saturday evening, April 18, and on the Monday and Tuesday evenings following, with the consultation on Wednesday. McLaren would need to arrive Saturday and could depart Thursday. He talked with Rose and Laren about the offers at lunch on Monday. "In a way I'm excited. These are my first offers from out of the country, but I have a problem in another way. I'll have to miss a full weekend with Sue."

"Don't be silly, McLaren. One weekend is a big step in your career. Do you know how Inverness figures into your personal history?"

McLaren laughed. "Momma, don't you constantly tell me to settle down and get married? Aren't you a little inconsistent?"

"I'm your momma. I can be as inconsistent as I want to be."

McLaren laughed again, "You're probably right about the weekend. I have plenty of time to explain to Sue—what's that noise?"

No one answered McLaren's question, but Laren went to the door and opened it. Celeste and Tim trembled outside. Celeste talked fast. "May we come in?"

Rose answered, "Sure, come in here. What's up?"

Celeste continued to talk fast. "I heard on the radio Roy escaped from prison in Illinois yesterday. They don't know where he is, but I know where he's headed. He's coming here to kill me. I don't want Roy to kill you too, but do you know where we can go to hide?"

Laren responded, "Aren't you supposed to be at work? Won't the guys at the factory protect you?"

"Yes, me, but they won't allow Tim in the factory because of safety rules. So I came home, grabbed him, and here we are."

"We're not afraid of Roy Simms. He probably figures everybody expects him to come here, so he'll go somewhere else." Laren smiled and welcomed, "You can stay here, though, until they catch him."

"He won't go somewhere else. He'll come here and kill me. He'll kill you too if you get in his way."

"Don't worry about it, because we won't." Laren turned to look at Rose. "Can you make a pallet on the floor in the living room like you did when Celeste stayed before?"

"Sure Laren." Rose paused. "I think I see somebody at the west house!"

Celeste looked out the window and screamed, "That's him. He'll kill me!"

Laren spoke to Rose. "Shut her up if you can. We don't want the guy to know she's over here."

McLaren held Celeste's arms, Rose put her hand over Celeste's mouth, and partly muffled the screams. Laren ran to the telephone. "I gotta call the sheriff. He set the west house afire." Laren made the telephone call and then exclaimed, "He's coming over here with a gas can! Forget about Celeste, McLaren, and get the rifle. We may have to shoot the guy."

"The rifle's in the barn, Poppa."

"Oh. When he gets even with the well, let's storm out and rush'im. We can't let'im burn us out and pick us off one at a time."

"Right, Poppa. I'll go first."

"Nope, I will. You ready?"

"Yeah."

"OK—NOW!"

Laren and McLaren jumped on Roy before he saw them coming. He turned out to be unarmed, but put up a major fight. The Patersons struggled several seconds to subdue him, and McLaren yelled, "Tim, you know where the lead rope in the barn is?"

"Yeah, McLaren, I'll bring it."

Tim ran out of the house and halfway to the barn before McLaren yelled, "Be careful."

Tim helped the Patersons tie Roy's feet together and his hands together behind his back, but McLaren stood with one foot on Roy's neck even after they tied him. Laren opined it was too late to try to put out the fire across the road. "We might as well let it burn."

Tim lunged toward the west house, but Laren grabbed him. Tim yelled, "Let me go. My science project's in there." Laren didn't say anything, but tightened his grip on Tim, who stopped trying to get away when the burning roof collapsed.

A sheriff's car arrived after a time. A man jumped out of the car and used a minimum of words to identify himself as Deputy Bill Shields. He glanced at the man tied on the ground and asked Laren to explain. Laren did, the deputy went to his mobile radio, and talked briefly. The deputy came back and looked west. "Looks like a total loss." He put handcuffs on Roy, removed the rope, and gave it to McLaren. He promised, "I'll take this guy off your hands," pushed him in the car, and drove toward Rounder.

Laren looked at McLaren. "I'm glad you're here, Son, because I couldn't do that myself. I guess the deputy helped some, but he showed up late. He didn't say much, did he?"

McLaren replied, "I can't stop shaking. We may've almost died. We need to go in and report to Celeste."

Celeste spoke from behind him. "You don't have to report to me. I saw it all. He'd have burned us up in the house except for you guys. I hope they lock him in the most secure cell they have this time."

"Celeste, everything you had burned in that house." McLaren shook his head and frowned.

"Yes, I have no idea what I'll do. Tim and I might have been better off if Roy had killed us."

Rose almost yelled, "Nonsense Celeste. We'll find clothes for you both. You can stay with us a day or so until we find a better place for you to live, and in the meantime you can work on a list of what you lost. Rounder people'll replace as much of it as possible."

McLaren added, "Yes, and Tim can eat with us and sleep in my room however long he needs to."

Rose seconded McLaren's offer. "That's for sure Celeste. I know you have a lot on your mind now, but Tim's somebody you don't need to worry about."

Celeste wobbled a second, then fell face forward onto the hood of McLaren's truck. Laren and McLaren carried her back in the house and put her in a chair, where she recovered.

Laren glanced toward the site of the west house. "I guess we don't need it. We'll miss Celeste's rent, but that's all we lost. It's as nothing compared to what Celeste lost."

McLaren grinned. "Bad things happen when I'm around. Roy Simms only comes when I'm here. Nobody ever sees a west house problem except me. I'm the one person Momma lectures about girls."

Rose smiled too. "Yes, you're a big problem. But I don't know what we'd do without you."

Laren looked at his new wristwatch and proclaimed it four o'clock and time to do chores. He and McLaren and Tim headed for the barn, while Rose made a pallet for Celeste and then prepared supper.

Celeste wore Rose's clothes to work on Tuesday. They didn't fit perfectly, but Rose laundered the clothes Celeste wore on Monday, and she wore them again Wednesday. A group of people from Rounder Church gathered more and better clothes by Thursday than Celeste lost in the fire. Tim didn't mind wearing the same clothes for several days, but the church group found clothes for him too. A Rounder builder said he had a small, trashed apartment he could recondition for Celeste. She had to stay with the Patersons six days, until the builder readied the apartment, and Tim could have crowded into it also, but he said he preferred to live with the Patersons. Celeste gave permission, and he stayed. Roy went back to Illinois and officials there assured Celeste they would hold on to him this time.

McLaren went to Kansas City to take Sue to supper at a restaurant the Friday after the fire. He knocked on her door and she ran out onto the front porch talking and opening her arms to hug. "Celeste called me yesterday. You're a real hero. Celeste says you saved Tim and her from certain death."

"Poppa and I may have."

"Don't try to be modest, McLaren. Celeste told me all about it."

"I'll accept any praise you want to give me, Sue, but we only did what we thought we had to do."

"Yes, right. Say whatever you want, but I know the truth."

Sue and McLaren had supper, and then went to Rounder to watch Tim play in a park-sponsored youth basketball league. The league reserved the high school gym, and while walking through the parking lot at the high school, Sue exclaimed, "There's Skip Barnes! Let's hurry and talk to him."

"You know Skip?"

"Oh, yes. He's a year younger than me, but Celeste baby-sat him when he was a boy." Sue yelled, "Hey, Skip!"

Chapter 20
1963 – 1964

Skip turned and waited when Sue called to him. "Hello, Sue. Hey, Muck. I hear you had a little fire out at your place this week."

"Yes, we—"

"I hear you tried to be a hero."

"Not really, Skip, but—"

"What's it like jumpin' on somebody when it's two on one?"

"Not much of a challenge, Skip. We have to go now." McLaren took Sue's arm and tried to guide her past Skip.

Skip jumped ahead, pointed to Sue, and snickered, "I suppose you told her all about the amazing heroic stuff you did."

Sue questioned, "What's the matter with you, Skip? I don't understand."

"They ain't much to understand, Sue. Wonder boy here thinks he's better'n everybody because he went to college, that's all." Skip pushed McLaren, much as he did years before at Number Five.

"Come on, Sue. Let's go back and sit in the truck awhile. We don't need trouble here." McLaren still had Sue's arm and he turned her around and they walked toward McLaren's vehicle.

Skip called after them, "Wonder boy—Muck—is a real hero, ain't he?" He shrugged and continued his earlier walk toward the gym.

McLaren opened the passenger door for Sue, helped her in, then went around the truck and slid into the driver's seat. Sue inquired, "What's the matter with Skip? Why did you let him chase us away like that?"

"Skip always resented me, Sue, from our days together in elementary school. I don't know why."

"You're not afraid of him?"

"No, of course not. But Skip and I are both in our mid-twenties. We're too old to fight like school boys."

"You only embolden him when you walk away."

"What do you think I should've done back there, Sue?" McLaren's voice betrayed his annoyance.

"I don't know. How long do you plan to sit here?"

"Maybe we can go on in now. Are you suggesting I should look for him and sit next to him?"

"No, silly."

"Come to think of it, maybe that's exactly where I want to sit. Are you game for that?"

"Yes, if you are."

McLaren and Sue entered the gym before the game began. McLaren scanned the bleachers for Skip and found him halfway up, near the middle. Their eyes met, Skip curled his lip, and stared at McLaren. He and Sue climbed the bleachers and found a place to sit, with McLaren adjacent to Skip. Skip didn't speak at all throughout the game, and McLaren talked only to Sue. Tim's team lost by a big margin, and Skip left about a minute before the end of the contest. McLaren and Sue waited for Tim to shower, dress, and return to the gym floor. They talked with Tim and his mom a few minutes, and then walked with them to the parking lot. They saw Skip with a group of his friends, but nobody spoke. Celeste and Tim drove away, and then McLaren and Sue did. Sue talked about the imbroglio on the way back to Kansas City. "I don't understand Skip. I didn't see that side of him when Celeste baby-sat him as a little boy."

"Did your family live in Rounder?"

"Yes, we were all Westigs then. I'm the only Westig left since Celeste married Roy. Where did you meet Skip?"

"I met him in school. He was a year ahead of me."

"Did you always run from him like you did tonight?"

"I didn't run from him tonight—or ever. Did you see anybody run tonight?"

"Not literally, but you came pretty close. If you don't stand up to him, he'll never stop."

"Whatever." McLaren didn't speak for the remainder of the trip to Kansas City. He dropped Sue off and came home early.

Rose asked at breakfast Saturday, "Did you and Sue have fun last night?"

"Not really, Momma. I may stay home tonight instead of driving all the way to Kansas City to see her."

Tim blurted, "What?"

Rose repeated, "What? Why?"

"No reason, Momma. I think I'll let her sit a couple of weeks."

Rose frowned. "McLaren, if you 'let her sit' you risk losing her. Why do you say that?"

"No reason. She's too bossy, that's all."

"How you treat her is up to you, but if your Poppa treated me that way, we'd have words. And the words wouldn't be sweet nothings!"

Laren grinned and confirmed to McLaren, "She's telling you the truth, Son."

McLaren ignored Laren. "Sue and I aren't remotely equivalent to you and Poppa."

"And if you 'let her sit,' you never will be."

"Do you really think you need to manage my social life?"

"Somebody needs to do it for you, McLaren."

Tim defended McClaren. "Aunt Sue's nice, Mrs. Paterson, but I like McLaren better, don't you?"

"Well, yes, Tim. I—well, maybe I said enough already. You men go on out to your chores. You too, Tim. Today's Saturday and I have work here in the house."

Sue called McLaren on the telephone Saturday after lunch, but they talked only a minute or so. McLaren didn't go to Kansas City that evening, but took Tim to a picture show in Rounder.

Celeste settled into her new apartment, and a few days later McLaren remarked to Rose, "You said something back before the new year about my personal history at Inverness. What did you mean?"

"Don't you know where your Grandpoppa and Grandmomma Paterson lived before they came here?"

"They rarely mentioned it. Somewhere in Scotland, right?"

"Yes, somewhere in Scotland, and to be specific, outside Inverness in Scotland."

"Hmm, that's interesting. Maybe I can see their former house while I'm there."

"It might be a pile of rubble. They didn't tell your poppa or me details either, but I think it wasn't much. Did you ever hear about it?"

"No."

"It could've been bad. They clammed up when asked about it. Your Poppa might know more than I do, but he probably doesn't."

"Do you know where it is?"

"Somewhere west, but that's all they ever said."

"Maybe Pastor Westerson knows. I'll ask him."

"Take your Kodak. You'll want pictures if you find it, and we'll want to see them."

Sue called McLaren again Thursday evening after the Skip Barnes confrontation, and this time they talked almost fifteen minutes. McLaren invited her out on Friday, but she had to play in her church orchestra. They went out Saturday, however, and McLaren came home late. Rose asked the next morning if they had fun, but McLaren didn't answer.

McLaren filled his speaking schedule for 1964 before January ended, and signed a contract to supervise a grounds update for a large factory in Kansas City. He dated Sue on weekends, and commuted from the farm to the factory job a few days, but boarded an airplane bound for New York and Inverness on Friday, April 17. Pastor Westerson met him at the Inverness airport Saturday afternoon, showed him the auditorium where he would speak, waited for him to check in at his hotel, and then took him out to the edge of town to see Tiny Kirk. McLaren interrogated the Pastor when they arrived at the kirk. "Did you meet my grandparents, Erroll and Kenzie Paterson?"

"No, they left the Highlands before I moved to Inverness with my parents."

"Did you ever hear about them?"

"Yes, some Tiny Kirk people mentioned them to me a few times."

"Did they join Tiny Kirk?"

"Not as far as I know, but they support us every year with endowment proceeds of nearly 1500 pounds."

"I didn't know they had that kind of money. How much is that in American dollars?"

"I'm not sure, but maybe around seven thousand."

"All that for this kirk? I wonder why they chose this one?"

"I can answer that one. They chose it because the Tiny Kirk food wagon fed them and their people each year. They explained they wanted to help Tiny Kirk continue and expand that ministry." Pastor Westerson continued. "Tiny Kirk fed them and received money before I came here, but the early 'food wagon' amounted to only one wagon; it went out once a year in a loop west and south of here, and the kirk focused on a one-time feeding. We changed that in recent years, partly because we can count on income from the Paterson endowment. We still make the original loop, plus two others, but our work now is more in the food pantry area. We solicit donations and offer food year-round, here in Inverness, and all along our loop routes."

"That's truly impressive, Pastor. Do you administer the food program?"

"No, the kirk established a board of trustees when the Paterson endowment first came in. Do you have time to get out of the car and look around the kirk before you go?"

"Sure. I should take off pretty quick, though, and go back to the hotel. I'll rent a car and go over my notes before I drive to the auditorium."

McLaren and the pastor walked all the way around the kirk and then returned to the hotel. The entire Inverness trip went fast, but lasted longer than McLaren wanted to be away from Sue. He postponed his departure, nevertheless.

He called Sue on the telephone at her work, Tuesday afternoon before his third speech in Inverness. "Hey, this is McLaren, calling to—"

"Oh, McLaren, I miss you. I try to work here, but fear I mostly count the hours, instead."

"Exactly the same here, but I want to look around more, and will stay another day. I expect to land in Kansas City on Friday instead of Thursday. Will you call Momma and tell her?"

"Sure, McLaren. So I have to count twenty-four more hours than I thought?"

"Maybe, but I don't want you to count more than necessary. May I pick you up at home about an hour after you get off work?"

"You can pick me up as little as a half hour after."

"Great, Sue. I'll see you at 4:30 on Friday then. If my plane's on time I'll have to wait a few hours, but that only means I won't be late. Do you want to go to The Golden Ox over by the stockyards and eat steak for supper, then go up north to River Front Road, where we can look across the river, sit in my truck, and talk for a while?"

"Sounds perfect, McLaren. So I should tell your momma you'll be home late?"

"Yes, tell her late. I must go now. My speech begins in an hour. I love you."

"McLaren! That's the first time you told me you love me!"

"Well, I do, and I can't wait to tell you in person."

"I love you too, McLaren, and I can't wait either."

"Bye, Sue. I love you."

McLaren made his third speech and consulted at Tiny Kirk the next day. He drove around the Inverness area Thursday, shopped some, and arrived in Kansas City on Friday. His plane landed two hours late, but he waited another two before he picked up Sue. They enjoyed steak and small talk before McLaren drove to a road overlooking the river. The vehicle engine barely stopped before Sue demanded, "Tell me about your trip before I die of curiosity."

McLaren told Sue about Tiny Kirk, their food pantry, and his recommendations to enhance the small grassy area around the kirk. He moved on to mention the speeches, and talked at length about the impression his grandparents made. "Several people waited to talk privately after every single speech. A few wanted to talk about landscape design, or whatever, but most wanted to talk about my grandparents and told me amazing things I never knew."

"Like what?"

"Most who talked to me thanked me for huge amounts of money my grandparents gave them. One older guy said he drove over a hundred km—I don't know how far that is, but he made it seem a long way—to meet me. He said my grandparents gave an endowment to his parents, enough he and his sister paid for their college and he paid startup expenses for a construction business he owns now. Others talked about huge grants that changed their forebears' lives; some of them even said people in their backgrounds knew my great grandpoppa. Most of them told me about things my grandparents or great grandpoppa did for old folks in their families before the money came. I felt about an inch high. I did nothing for any of those people, but they treated me as a really big deal."

"You are a really big deal, McLaren, but I thought of your grandparents as poor people. I never heard anybody say otherwise."

"Yes, and it's a big mystery to me too, Sue. Part of the reason I took an extra day is I wanted to drive around the Scottish Highlands. It's beautiful country, and my grandparents surely had an idyllic life there. I went out west, where Pastor Westerson thinks they lived, and didn't see any old houses or ruins. I saw a huge stone office building and a fabulous body of water called Beauty Firth, and they were impressive, but I didn't see anything else of note. I didn't question my grandparents about where they lived, and I regret it now that I've been close to the spot. But about them being rich—they clearly had to be, to give away as much money as people say they did. I think they accumulated it there, because it couldn't have happened on eighty acres in rural Jake County."

"Do your parents know about their Scottish origins?"

"No, they were born in Jake County. I once asked Momma, but she didn't know anything. I did want to talk to you about my trip, but that's not the most important reason I asked you here."

"What is that reason McLaren?"

"We have to get out of the truck." McLaren walked around the front of the pickup and opened the door for Sue. He dropped to one knee before she had both feet on the ground.

"Oh yes! I will!"

"You will what? I haven't asked you anything yet!"

"I will marry you! If you ask me anything else, I'll drag you into the river!"

"I have a ring, all the way from Inverness. You want it?"

"I'm saying yes to everything, McLaren. Yes! You're what I most want, but I do want the ring. I'm thrilled you told me you love me. I love you too, and can't wait to marry. I bet we can find a preacher tonight!"

Chapter 21
1964

"I'm in a hurry to marry too, but maybe we should think about where we'll live. We have to decide whether to live close to the farm or close to your work."

"Let's live in Rounder. I don't care that much about my job, and while we look for a place to live, I can look for a job there. Let's get back in the truck. Mosquitos are eating me up."

"OK, I'm ready to get back in, and Rounder's best for me and probably for Tim. I already know where the 'For Rent' signs are, and on top of that, Momma's a friend of Sharon D'Arliss of Rounder Realty. Kansas City's bigger, but we can probably find a place in Rounder faster. Where do you want the wedding?"

"I don't care about a wedding. I want a marriage and I want it quick."

"Same here. How about Rounder Church, with nobody present except my parents, Celeste, and Tim?"

"I like that, McLaren, but shouldn't we be there too?"

"Touch'e! Maybe Pastor Thomas, too. So when?"

"Do we have to wait until we know about a place to live and my job?"

"Not by my lights. Can we say a week from Saturday?"

"Yes we can, McLaren. I'll give notice to the library and to my landlord tomorrow or Monday."

They sat close together in the truck and talked until the wee hours. McLaren took Sue home, and later tried to sneak into his bedroom at the farm, but had to go through Rose and Laren's room to get to his west room. He awakened them, as well as Tim, but didn't talk to anyone until breakfast-time the next day.

McLaren went immediately to his important announcement at breakfast. "I asked Sue to marry me last night, and she said yes."

Rose smiled. "I thought maybe you did when you came in so late. It's about time for you to give that poor girl some certainty."

"We plan to marry at Rounder Church a week from today. Can you be there?"

Rose wrinkled her brow. "Oh, McLaren! I don't know if I can get ready that soon."

"Momma, you don't need to get ready. Sue and I'll take care of it. All we want you and Poppa to do is show up."

"People don't marry that way nowadays, McLaren. I need more time to do it right."

Laren interjected, "Maybe you should let the boy alone, Rose. It's his wedding."

Tim begged, "Can I go?"

Rose answered, "Of course, Tim."

McLaren added, "We want you there most of all, Tim. We couldn't have a wedding without you, and you can bring your mom too."

Rose grumbled most of the day about not having time, not being consulted, and generally being left out. Her complaints included, "There won't be time for me to put an announcement in the paper or for people to buy gifts."

McLaren shook his head. "We don't want the paper to announce anything. We don't want gifts. We don't want you to do anything whatsoever, except be there. I don't know how to make it more clear to you."

McLaren helped Laren early in the day, but left in the middle of the afternoon to go see Sue. He brought her back to Rounder, where they found an apartment before night. They went to the farm for supper. McLaren told his parents the location of the apartment and informed Rose, "Sue and I'll eat most meals, at least breakfast and supper, at our new home in Rounder after we're married."

"Why don't you both come out here for all your meals? Tim's out here, and there's no reason for you to pay good money for food when we have more than we can eat right here."

"I appreciate that, Momma, and I'm sure Sue does too, but it'll be quicker and easier to eat where we live. And besides," McLaren grinned, "we're in love." He continued, "I did outfox myself though. I only signed one contract for this summer, and chose Kansas City, because that's where Sue lives. But we'll soon live in Rounder, so Kansas City's no better than any other place."

McLaren and Sue walked past the barn, down the bluff, and to their favorite sitting log to talk, after supper on Friday. They planned details of their life in exact and unrealistic detail. They talked about a delayed honeymoon, about a possible trip together to Scotland, and about the three children Sue said she wanted. They worried about the big glitch in their plans, namely uncertainty about McLaren's life work. "I enjoy travel to help people beautify their grounds, Sue. But at the same time, I feel I should stay here, take the load off Poppa, and be the father Tim doesn't have. I can't decide if I'm an eagle and should soar over the world, or if I'm a groundhog and should stay here and burrow."

"I love you, McLaren, and it doesn't matter to me whether you're an eagle or a groundhog. Maybe you can talk about your future with your parents."

"I have. They say be the eagle. They'll sacrifice for me, but I don't know if I should ask them to do it. Poppa says I'll let people down in other cities if I don't go, and he's right. But I'll let him down if I go. I feel needed to the point it's almost a curse, and threatens to pull me apart. I don't want to let people down far away, and I don't want to let people down at home. I can't learn more from Baird—he and I sat on a log near this very spot and talked about me looking for gold here. He persuaded me true happiness comes from producing things people need, but different people need different things."

"Will it work to make Poppa a partner in your landscaping business, just as he made you a partner in the farm?"

"I thought about that, Sue, but Poppa'd see it as a gift, almost like charity, and he's too independent for that."

"Can you be *both* the eagle and the groundhog?"

"Did you ever see a groundhog fly, or an eagle burrow?"

"You're more than an eagle or a groundhog McLaren. You're a human being with more capacity to think, to adapt, and to do. I think you can do both."

"I've tried to do both, but when I do one, I neglect the other."

"Every mother struggles with a similar problem, McLaren. Different mothers respond in different ways, and maybe some just muddle through. I think you can muddle with the best, or more likely, rise above muddle. I don't know what you should do, but I think you'll figure it out. Have you prayed about it?"

"Not much. I'll do it. But first," McLaren stood, "I'll race you to the truck."

They arrived at the truck out of breath, after everybody else went to bed. McLaren took Sue home, returned to Kansas City for her on Sunday afternoon, and again after her work on Monday and Tuesday. She found a job with a carpet cleaning company on Tuesday, but McLaren argued against the job. "You don't have to work. I make plenty of money—as eagle or as groundhog—so you can stay at home full time if you wanta do that."

"Yes, I know I can, but I'll go bananas in our little apartment unless I do more than take care of it. My concern isn't that I think you don't make enough money; I need to work for my own wellbeing. Shall we move my stuff to our new apartment before the wedding?"

"Not in my opinion, Sue. Our wedding's scheduled for ten o'clock Saturday, so we'll have time afterward to get our stuff—both yours and mine—in the afternoon. I won't look again at the Kansas City jobsite until Monday, so we'll have Saturday night and Sunday to settle in."

McLaren took Sue back to Kansas City early Tuesday evening, and drove by his former gas station, Rounder Service, on his way home. While Skip pumped his gas and before he had time to be rude, McLaren commented, "We need to talk about why we argue so much, Skip."

Skip sneered. "The reason's plain. You're an uppity muckity muck."

"What do you mean by that?"

"We close at ten, and it's about eight 'till now. If you hang around, I'll give you an ear full, a face full, or whatever you want, when we close."

McLaren paid for the gas, drove across the street, parked his truck, walked back to Rounder Service, stood by a gas pump, and waited. The owner of the gas station left a couple minutes before ten. Skip turned off the lights, locked the doors, and turned to McLaren. "What exactly is it you want?"

"The real question is, what do you want, Skip?"

Skip growled, "Looks like a standoff. You may not know what you want, but I know what you need, and if you bug me, I'll see you get it."

"What are you mad about, Skip?"

"I ain't mad, Muck, you're the uppity one."

"You think I'm uppity?"

"Ain't you?"

"Why would I be uppity?"

"Beats me. You tell me."

"What makes you think that?"

"You got the big college degree. You got the big bucks. You got the new truck, the big farm, the old ladies sayin' you're great. You think them sayin' it makes it so, but it don't."

"Does it bother you that you don't have a college degree?"

"It don't bother me none. I'm glad I ain't got one, because I don't want to act like you."

"You can have a college degree if you wanta work for it Skip. You can get a scholarship if money's a problem. I can help you with the money part."

"Yeah, there you go again." Skip affected a different tone of voice. "I can help you with the money part." His voice returned to his normal tone. "You think you're hot stuff, don't you?"

McLaren turned away. "Nobody can stop you if you want to whine and complain, but if you get tired of it and want to change, let me know. I can help you, and I will if you tell me you're ready for it." McLaren walked back across the street, climbed in his truck, and drove back to the farm.

Saturday morning arrived. McLaren picked up Sue at her place in Kansas City a couple hours early, along with a few of her belongings. They went to Rounder, put her things in the apartment, and drove to Rounder Church a half hour before ten. Celeste, Tim, and McLaren's parents arrived a few minutes later; Pastor Thomas suggested they go ahead with the ceremony. They did, and McLaren and Sue walked out of the church, married, before ten o'clock. The entire group stood and talked a few minutes, then everybody headed out to the farm to pick up McLaren's clothes, radio, and alarm clock. They all stayed for lunch, then McLaren and Sue dropped off McLaren's stuff at the apartment and returned to Kansas City for the remainder of her things. They returned to their Rounder apartment at four, and didn't come back out until Sunday morning.

The new couple went to Rounder Church, then took Celeste to the farm for Sunday dinner, and remained until midafternoon. They returned to the apartment in Rounder and stayed inside until Monday morning. They talked at breakfast before they each went to work. Sue inquired, "How long will you work on the Kansas City job?"

"Pretty much all summer, but not all day every day. The grounds amount to a short seven acres, so I have a lot to think about. I mapped it all before I went to Inverness, and thought about it, but that's about all. I'll sit here on Tuesday and Wednesday to write out a preliminary plan. Factory management wants to look at the plan and we already set an appointment for Thursday morning for that. They might want changes and I can't predict how long we'll go back and forth on a plan. When do you expect to be home tonight?"

"About 4:30, and you better be here too." Sue grinned.

"Oh, Sue, I'm sorry, but I probably won't. I haven't helped Poppa with chores for several days, and I wanta show him I'm still alive. I'll go out to help today."

"McLaren, you can't be gone—we're newlyweds after all! When will you be back?"

"I can't say for sure, Sue, but I have to do it. I should be back by 5:30 if Poppa doesn't send me off to another project."

Sue pouted, "How long will you need for the actual work at the factory?"

"That's the part that could go on most of the summer, but I only have to supervise it. Part of my plan is to name subcontractors, so when management signs off on the plan, they'll sign off on the subcontractors too. Poppa'll cut hay sometime in late May, and I want to help him with that as much as I can, and will also need to guide the factory work at least a few hours most days. I wish I didn't have to work, but I do. Didn't you know that all along?"

"Can't you spend more time here with me? Tim's thirteen now, and should be able to help with the hay."

"Yeah, Tim's already as good a tractor driver as Poppa or me, and he can unload hay onto the elevator, but he's still a little light to load wagons or stack hay in the barn. He's good help now and will be better in a few years. Poppa, on the other hand, is sixty and needs us both. He already plays out sooner than he did ten years ago, and he may go downhill about as fast as Tim comes on. Tim'll be about ready to go off to college when he hits his peak, so his labor will drop from most of what we need, down to nothing. I want to please you, Sue, but I think I'll always be stuck with work."

"Don't worry about college. I'm sure Tim won't go, because Celeste can't afford it."

"Yes, but we can. I already have enough money in a college fund for Tim, sitting there waiting for him."

"You do? I didn't know about that—I don't think Celeste knows either."

"Nobody knows. Not Tim, not my parents, not Celeste, not anybody . . . or at least not anybody except you."

"I don't know why you didn't tell me before now, but better late than never I guess. You should—you must—tell Tim and Celeste too. I have no idea if it matters to Celeste, but it could influence what classes Tim selects in high school. I'll tell 'em if you don't, because they need to know. Maybe you should tell Laren too. He ought to know ahead of time if Tim intends to leave the farm for college."

"Go ahead and tell 'em if you think I can't do it. Maybe I should tell you something else—I don't want us to argue over money, especially money that's not even ours. But on top of Tim's money, we have more 'n we can spend, and can afford for you to start to college this fall. Are you interested in that?"

"I don't think I am. How will it benefit us?"

"Us isn't who you should think about."

"I do think about us, and I can't think of a benefit."

"The only reason I studied horticulture in college is that I liked it. I didn't see a particular use for it beyond our kitchen gardens on the farm, but it prepared me to establish an interesting and decently profitable business—as well as to create the eagle/groundhog problem."

"Yes, but I don't want a business and I don't think I can be either an eagle or a groundhog."

"So you might want to know things purely for your own pleasure? Or to qualify for jobs, like doctor, teacher, or social worker?"

"I already have as much pleasure as I can stand—or I would if you'd stay home—and I don't want any of those jobs."

"You don't have to decide today, Sue, but you can think about it."

"Yes, I'll do that, but don't look for a change."

"That's for you to decide, but if you choose to do it, we can put the entire payment for the Kansas City job into it. Money isn't one of our problems."

"How did we get off on college? All I asked you was how long the Kansas City job will take."

"If I don't leave the apartment and head up there, it may take longer'n I thought! I'll see you sometime this evening. Bye."

The factory manager at Kansas City professed a landscaping objective when he signed the original contract, but a different one when they met on Thursday. McLaren insisted on a new contract before he continued, and the dustup over that set the expected completion date back two weeks.

McLaren discussed the revised date with Sue at supper one evening in May. "We planned our honeymoon to begin in early August, but with the new contract, I won't be free in time for our honeymoon then."

"Is that a problem, McLaren? Why can't we postpone the honeymoon and you stay home more? I think every day I'm married to you is a honeymoon. We can't make our life better if we label a couple of weeks a honeymoon, can we?"

"The timing is crucial if you go to college this fall."

"Did I ever say I plan to go to college?"

"You didn't, but Celeste did. She says you told her you want to go to Jakesville this fall, to study dietetics and nutrition."

"Oh, that. Yes, maybe sometime, but it doesn't have to be this year."

"If you want to do it, then it does have to be this year. Maybe we could have our honeymoon during your Christmas break from classes."

"Sure, McLaren. Like I said, I don't need a honeymoon, but if we have one, it can be any time; I'm not particular."

"The only problem is, we have to persuade Momma to have her Christmas celebration early, so we don't miss it and make her mad. Do you think she'll do it?"

"I know she will, McLaren. But don't wait to ask her until two days before."

"I don't like to ask you to change, or Momma either, and I wouldn't if the factory manager knew his mind."

"It's all right with me, and I know with Momma too. Did Skip ever call you?"

"Skip?"

"Skip Barnes. He called here minutes after you left for the factory this morning. He said he must talk to you. I supposed he called you at the factory; maybe you should call him."

"OK, I will. Or maybe I'll go down to Rounder Service, because I think that's where he is. I'll walk over there now."

McLaren arrived soon at Rounder Service and found Skip walking with a slight limp. "Hey, Skip. Sue said you called."

"Yeah, Muck—McLaren. I'll tell the boss I'm off the clock for a few minutes—can I ask you something?"

"Of course, Skip, anything."

"You go to church don't you?"

"Sure, down at Rounder Church."

"Will you pray for me?"

Chapter 22
1964 – 1965

"I already pray for you a lot, Skip. Do you ask for a particular reason?"

"I have a sore on my foot and it's been there for months. Doc says he'll have to cut the foot off if it gets worse. Will you pray about that?"

"You know it, Skip. Should we start now?"

"No, somebody might see us. But I'll appreciate it if you pray real hard. I don't want nobody to cut my foot off."

"I'll pray on the way home, Skip, will ask Sue to join me, and will ask Pastor Thomas, Momma, Poppa—"

"Whoa, hold on. I don't want nobody to know."

"God hears a single voice, Skip, but many might be better."

"How about if you tell Sue and nobody else? And make sure Sue don't talk?"

"You're the boss, Skip. Sue or I won't talk unless you turn us loose."

"Good. You won't forget will you?"

"Never."

"I gotta get back on the clock. Thanks, McLaren."

McLaren went home, told Sue, asked her not to tell, and they prayed for Skip immediately and often.

They bought a two-year-old Rambler Classic sedan, because McLaren still needed his truck every day, and Sue also needed a vehicle. McLaren kept his factory work on schedule, and the factory manager signed a completion certificate on August 31; Sue quit her carpet-cleaning job to enter college at Jakesville. They continued to pray for Skip, and although he said his foot didn't get worse, he said it didn't get better. He asked McLaren to continue to pray.

McLaren had more time during the fall and early winter, and helped Laren with both morning and evening chores almost every day. He had more time to talk with both his parents and told Sue he longed to ask them to help pray for Skip, and would have, but Skip wanted secrecy.

The normal pattern of early calls for next year continued in December of 1964, and McLaren accepted speaking jobs in Atlanta, Boise, and Wilmington before Sue's Christmas break, but turned down two landscape offers. Callers scattered the speaking engagements among the first three months of the year, but he hoped to fill in the gaps with more. He rejected the landscape offers because they were too far from Rounder, but had no other offers by Sunday, December 20, the day Rose scheduled the Paterson Christmas get-together. Celeste and Tim attended, along with Baird and family, and McLaren enjoyed seeing them all. Winter weather crowded everybody into the house, but McLaren saw the togetherness as a plus. Baird and Maye's children came with them, maybe the last time for Joseph, because he expected to graduate from high school in the spring. Rose and Laren enjoyed the day more than anybody; McLaren later admitted to Sue, however, some of the tales about old times grew a bit from one year to the next.

Baird's family left for Boston on Monday the twenty-first, and McLaren and Sue left for Florida and their twice-delayed honeymoon the same day. They stopped for gas at Rounder Service on their way to the Kansas City airport. Skip put the gas in their car and then asked them to pull around back for a minute, where he took off his shoe and sock and showed them his foot. "The last time Doc looked— Thursday—he said the foot looked some better. The red's less red since then, and the space covered is way less. Your prayin' worked, Muck! Don't stop now."

Skip put his shoe back on and Sue asked, "Why don't you go to Rounder Church Sunday and learn for yourself how to pray?"

"I went there yesterday, Sue. Didn't you see me?"

"Oh, Skip! How could I have missed you? No, I didn't see you."

"Maybe because I got there late, set in back, and cleared out early. But I intend on goin' back. I'll talk to you next time."

"I have to say 'oh' again, Skip. McLaren and I are on our way to Florida, and won't be there Sunday. We'll be there the next Sunday, though, and we'll look for you. In the meantime, we'll keep praying."

"See ya when ya get back."

McLaren and Sue enjoyed their visit to Florida, but less than they might have, because Sue worried about a paper for English class, and McLaren wanted to be back by the phone if a landscape offer came in.

They returned on Friday, December 31. They didn't need gas, but stopped at Rounder Service to check on Skip. He met them, and smiled. "I won't take my shoe off today, but this week's the first time my foot felt so good I forgot about it. Doc says it turned the corner a couple o' weeks ago. But don't stop prayin'."

Sue replied, "We'll never stop Skip, unless you tell us to stop."

She finished a rough draft of her paper on Saturday, but the telephone didn't ring for McLaren. Monday, however, the telephone rang off the hook, as McLaren described it. He accepted three more speaking jobs for January through March, and received two landscaping queries from the Kansas City area. He went out to the farm around four o'clock to help with chores, and left Sue alone to take the most interesting call of the day.

The telephone rang soon after McLaren left, and Sue heard, "Hello. This is Reginald Barker of Northwest Medical Office Spaces. Hello? Are you still there?"

"Yes, I'm here."

"I tried to call McLaren Paterson for a week."

"I'm here."

"Mr. Paterson there?"

"No he's out, but should be back soon."

"Who are you?"

"I'm Mrs. Paterson."

"Can you deliver a message to Mr. Paterson?"

"Certainly."

"Ask him if he'll straighten out our grounds here at Medical Office Spaces. They're a mess."

"When do you want him to do it?"

"Not in winter. Later, when summer comes."

"Shall I have him call you?"

Sue obtained a telephone number from Mr. Barker, wrote it on a paper, and assured him McLaren would call, probably before seven.

Barker asked, "Rounder time?"

"Yes."

McLaren returned from the farm, and Sue told him, "You had a call from Mr. Reginald Barker while you were gone. He's with Northwest Medical Office Spaces. I told him you'll return his call by seven Rounder time."

"Where is he?"

"At Northwest Medical Off—"

"I mean where in the US is he?"

"I don't know. I wrote down his telephone number. This is it." Sue gave McLaren the paper with the number on it.

"This looks like a number from outside the US. What's the guy want?"

"He says the grounds around the Office Spaces are a mess. He wants you to fix them."

"I don't wanta go out of the country."

"I told him you'll call."

"OK, I'll call, but I won't go out of the country." He called.

"Yes."

"I'm McLaren Paterson. My wife said you phoned."

"About a dozen times I'm afraid. Can you come this summer?"

"Come where to do what?"

"I'm sorry. I'm Reginald Barker of Northwest Medical Office Spaces."

"Yes. Where are those spaces?"

"West of the city."

"What city?"

"I'm sorry. Mrs. Paterson didn't give you a complete message, did she?"

"Mr. uh Barker, please don't criticize my wife. Do you want something from me?"

"I'm sorry again. Yes, can you straighten up our grounds?"

"You didn't tell me where those grounds are."

"West of Inverness, south of Beauty Firth."

"Oh, maybe I've seen your place. Is it an older stone building?"

"Yes, barely outside the city."

"What do you include in 'straighten up the grounds'?"

"Whatever it takes. We might need grading, new trees, new flowers, and a whole bunch of new grass."

"You might describe an ambitious project, Mr. Barker. I could need most of the summer and a boatload of money."

"I understand. Our tenants are doctors and health professionals. They can pay well, but won't if the place doesn't look up to snuff. We already lost a couple."

"I'm interested, Mr. Barker, but must talk with my wife. May I call you back tomorrow?"

"Absolutely."

"What time is it in Inverness?"

"It's 11:05 pm."

"So we have a five hour time difference? If I call you before noon here, I should catch you during business hours there?"

"Yes, any time's fine, but daytime's better."

"I'll call. Thanks."

McLaren hung up the telephone and turned to Sue. "Do you want to know where Barker is?"

"Do I?"

"West of Inverness. I probably drove past there last summer. When's your school out for the summer, and when's it start up in the fall?"

"I have to check, but classes began last year during the third week of August. We'll be out this spring in the second week of May."

"I really want that job, but only if you can go. We'll have to live in a hotel all summer, which will run up the cost, so Barker, or whoever he is, might decide to hire somebody local. If I can get the job and if it doesn't mess up your school, will you go? If I take that one, I'll have to turn the others down."

"Does the sun rise in the east? Of course I'll go! We had a honeymoon in Florida, but this will be like a longer one in Scotland. You can't stop me if you try."

McLaren grinned. "Don't worry, I won't try."

He worked out a schedule to include a Wednesday, May 12 departure and a Wednesday, August 18 return, then telephoned Mr. Barker the next day, gave a safely high tentative price, work dates based on his description of the work, and Barker agreed to it.

Chapter 23
1965

Sue's Christmas break had not ended when McLaren agreed to the Inverness job, so they both went out to see Rose immediately after he accepted.

"Guess what, Momma." McLaren grinned.

"I can see from your eyes you're fixing to tell me something good, so go ahead and do it. Don't make me guess."

"Sue and I plan to go back to Inverness next summer."

"Wonderful, McLaren. More speeches?"

"No to supervise a landscape job like the one I did in Kansas City last summer."

"Can't you find anything closer to home? Poppa'll miss you at hay hauling time."

"Yes, I feel terrible about that part. But the beautiful part is, it's somewhere near where Grandpoppa and Grandmomma Paterson lived. Maybe Sue and I together will learn more this time. Where's Poppa?"

"He's cutting ice for cows and should be back in here soon."

"Is Tim with him?"

"Yes, and I feel better that Tim's along when he walks on slick ice."

"Me too. Along with our Scotland trip, I'm up to five speeches in the first quarter. They're pretty scattered in time and place, but they pay way more than enough to cover plane travel. Maybe I can add a few speeches when people learn I'm in their area."

Sue and McLaren waited for Laren and Tim to come in, told them the news, and discussed summer work. "We'll be away all summer

Poppa, so I can't help you haul hay. I hate that, but accepted the Inverness job anyway."

"Don't worry about it, Son. I don't plan to do much hay work this summer. I'll hire some high school boys, and Tim can ramrod the whole thing. We'll do things the same as if you had a job in Kansas City or Jakesville."

"Thanks, Poppa. Did Grandpoppa or Grandmomma ever talk to you about exactly where they lived in Scotland?"

"No, they hardly mentioned it. Your great grandpoppa's buried over there you know, and I think they never got over that."

"Hey, I forgot about him. Maybe we can find his grave."

Laren smiled. "Are you going over there to work, or to chase around?"

"Maybe to work as little as possible and to chase around as much as we can." McLaren smiled too.

Rose admonished, "Now you don't mean that. You didn't build your business chasing around, but you can wreck it that way."

"You're right, Momma." McLaren laughed. "Sue's the problem— she's a bad influence on me."

"Don't laugh, McLaren. You tend to business over there."

"Right, Momma." McLaren's voice sounded contrite, but he couldn't hide another grin.

Sue rescued him. "I'll watch him, Momma. I'm serious, and down deep, he is too. I know he'll put the job ahead of everything. He will."

Sue and McLaren stayed for lunch, then went back to their apartment, where Sue finished her paper for English class, and McLaren made a preliminary map of the Office Spaces grounds from his recollection of Mr. Barker's description.

McLaren lectured in Wilmington and Philadelphia on separate trips in January. He spoke in Kansas City, Missouri; Kansas City, Kansas; and Independence, Missouri during February, and Boise and Atlanta in March. Sue didn't go to any of the cities because of her school, but McLaren accumulated enough money to pay for her second year of college. Skip Barnes became a regular at Rounder Church and a friend to McLaren and Sue. Skip decided the last Sunday in March to become a church pastor, and thus needed college. McLaren spoke to him about the cost. "If you need scholarship money, Skip, I know we can find it."

"The money ain't the problem, McLaren. Don't you know? I cain't read."

"Whoa, Bessie! No, I didn't know. How can you be a pastor if you can't—we have to fix that. Let me talk to Sue and I'll get back to you today. We have less than six—less than five months. Can I call you at home, or will you be at the station?"

"I'm scheduled in at the station, startin' at 1:30 today."

"I'll look for you there about ten minutes ahead of that, so you don't have to miss work."

McLaren almost ran away from Skip to talk to Sue. "Skip told me he can't read, but he plans to start college in August. Can he do it?"

"Wow, that's a shocker! I don't know if he can, McLaren. He'll have to be a near genius to get up to where he needs to be. If he does th—I don't think he can do it."

"We need to think of something fast. I told him I'll see him at the gas station at 1:20."

"We can't do that, McLaren. You know your Momma expects us for dinner, and she won't serve it until one or later. We can't suddenly just not show up."

"I didn't promise for you. Maybe you can stay with Momma and I can see Skip?"

"She'll be disappointed, McLaren."

"How about if we go home, explain, and say we'll be back as fast as we can?"

"Doesn't sound perfect to me, but perhaps we can't do better."

"Good, let's go straight out there and have as much time as we can."

Sue and McLaren went to the farm and had to wait a few minutes for Laren, Tim and Rose to arrive. McLaren explained as soon as they got out of their car. "Sue and I need to leave—for only a few minutes—but probably in the middle of dinner. We—"

Rose grimaced and begged, "Won't you have time to eat before you go? What can be more important than your Sunday dinner?"

Sue answered, "McLaren discovered Skip Barnes can't read, but we also know he wants to go to college this fall. He told Skip he'd have some ideas and talk to him at the station at 1:20, so we have a double problem, in that we have to leave early, and we don't have any ideas yet."

"Let's go inside. You can have your dessert first, because I made pies yesterday, and we can talk about Skip   why does he want to go to college? Our dinner'll be a little strung out because Celeste isn't here yet, but we can deal with it. Laren, you think of things while I set the table."

Sue explained why Skip needed college, and Laren turned to Tim. "You have a thought?"

"Not really, Mr. Paterson. My mom reads really good. She might know something when she gets here."

Sue's frown eased and she suggested, "Speaking of Celeste, she has a teacher friend at Rounder Elementary. I think her name's Cindy, and she teaches remedial reading. Perhaps Celeste will ask her."

McLaren shook his head. "Maybe, but that won't give us anything to tell Skip at 1:20."

Everybody looked at McLaren, but eventually Laren spoke. "Somebody like this Cindy girl, somebody who knows what she's doing, could be the best bet. You know anything better, McLaren?"

McLaren muttered, "No."

Sue continued, "Celeste should show up in a few minutes. Unless she knows somebody better than Cindy—well, if she does or doesn't, I think we should wait for her."

Rose broke in to announce, "Your pie's ready. I see Celeste's car now. We can have pie first, then I'll bring out the main meal, and maybe McLaren and Sue won't miss too much of it."

"Thanks, Momma. Maybe it'll turn out all right." McLaren smiled.

Celeste approved the Cindy suggestion and offered to listen to Skip practice when she could. Tim offered the same, then all the Patersons did too. McLaren and Sue were on time for their appointment with Skip, McLaren told about Cindy, and asked, "Is it OK with you if Celeste talks to her?"

"Yeah. Cindy Hicks?"

Sue nodded. "Yes, she's the one. You know her?"

"Yeah, Cindy came with Celeste sometimes when she babysat me years ago. Cindy's nice. Whatever you say, I'll try it."

"We'll ask Celeste to clear it with Cindy then, and she'll probably call you to set up an initial appointment. McLaren and I still worry about college costs. Do you want us to help you with that?"

"No, my boss says I can work flexible hours and fit them around classes at Jakesville."

McLaren frowned. "I don't know about that, Skip. You might work a little, but you need to go all out to make it in college, and Cindy may want you to spend a lot of time with her right away. You can't read a lick?"

"Maybe a little. I can read the Dick and Jane books, but not much more."

"Well, the next move's up to us. Sue, will you ask Celeste to contact Cindy?"

"Of course, so Skip, all you need to do for now is wait for Cindy to call you. We have to get back to the farm, but you know where we live, if anything comes up."

McLaren and Sue returned for Momma's dinner, and Celeste promised to talk to Cindy before the day ended.

Cindy met with Skip and did what she called a diagnostic test on him. She claimed he could be ready for college by August if he had reading aptitude, but she recommended he read a minimum of twenty hours per week. Because she met with him another hour each weekday, Skip had to reduce his work schedule from seventy-two hours a week to fifty immediately, and McLaren recommended he slash hours even more at the start of the college semester. "You can't believe how much time college takes. You don't merely attend classes, you need commute time and study time. Even twenty hours of work can be tough while you're in college."

"I can't cut back that much, McLaren. I have to work to pay for school and to support myself."

"Maybe Sue and I can figure ways to get the cost down, Skip. Let us work on that, and don't plan to buy a car to go to Jakesville, because you can ride with Sue. If you can't read fast enough when school starts, all of us Patersons will read to you, whatever you ask. I'm confident Tim and Celeste will, too."

McLaren tended his gardens at the farm and at the Rounder parks during the early part of the year and into May. He talked to Sue about the Inverness trip early in May. "I know we can't go until your school ends, and our plane tickets are for May 12, but I can hardly wait. These landscape jobs should be old hat to me, but this one's different, because of where it is."

"Yes I know how you feel. I never had relatives there but I'm probably as excited as you are."

"What will you do while we're there and I'm at work?"

"I'll stand over you with a big whip. I promised your Momma."

"No, I mean seriously?"

"I'll take some text books for next year, but probably won't open them. I'm sure I'll drive around the area and be a tourist part of the time. I might even go with you and watch how you do your work part of the time."

"Momma mentioned Great Grandpoppa Paterson is buried over there, and I want to find where that is if I do nothing else beyond work. That might tell us something about where he lived or what he did over there."

May 12 eventually arrived, and Sue and McLaren boarded their plane for New York and Inverness. They touched down at Inverness on Friday, May 14, rented a car, then a hotel room, and looked for the Office Spaces building. They found it quickly and McLaren confimed, "Yes, that's the building I remember. I wanta drive a mile or so farther, to show you Beauty Firth. Its name describes it well."

They saw the firth before they drove a mile. "You're right, McLaren. It's so beautiful it takes my breath away. Can you find a place to stop along here?"

He stopped the car and they admired the firth for several minutes before McLaren suggested, "I should turn the car around and go back to look at the Office Spaces grounds. I'll wait until Monday to start work, but it'll be nice to at least look today. Maybe I'll drive up in the parking lot and we can sit there a few minutes."

They arrived at the parking lot, and Sue remarked, "I see what Mr. Barker meant, McLaren. The building looks rundown, and it matches the grounds."

"Yes, I don't know if they plan anything for the building, but if they don't, I should probably try to hide it with tall trees. Let's go look for Tiny Kirk. I think I can find it—I told you about that, remember?"

"I remember, McLaren. I want to see the kirk and the lawn around it."

They easily found the kirk; it had new paint, and plants grew nearly as McLaren proposed a couple years earlier. They thought the kirk beautiful, but didn't stop. Instead, they went back to their hotel, enjoyed supper in a restaurant there, went up to their room, and retired for the night.

McLaren suggested they go back to Tiny Kirk and try to find Pastor

Westerson the next day, Saturday. They tried the door, but found it locked. They returned to their car, turned around in the parking lot, and saw an old man out back, weeding a flowerbed. McLaren rolled the car window down and called to him. "Sir? Sir?"

The man straightened up and walked to the car. "Can I help you?"

"Yes, my name is McLaren Paterson and—"

"Oh, you're Mr. Paterson. Yes. You're the guy we talked with about the flowers." He gestured toward them. "I remember you now. If you need anything at all, I'll—"

McLaren interrupted, "What's your name?"

"I'm Charles Roth. I volunteer on Saturdays to do outside work here at the kirk."

"We're glad to meet you, Mr. Roth. I think my family lived around here someplace back around the turn of the century. Do you have any idea where they lived?"

"I think they lived here before old man Smalley went to the asylum years ago, and I lived down by Edinburgh at the time. But people still talk about the Patersons. I think they were somehow connected to the Smalleys, and lived west of town somewhere."

"My great grandfather John Paterson might be buried someplace around here. Do you happen to know where?"

"I wish I did, but I don't."

"Can you suggest anybody who might know?"

"No. Everybody talks about the Patersons, and everybody agrees they did fine things, but nobody agrees about details. They supposedly lived a long time ago. I don't know where you can find anybody who really knows anything; I wish I did. I mow the Tiny Kirk cemetery in the summers, and there's nobody out there named Paterson. You might try other cemeteries in Inverness. They're probably all in the telephone book; we have a book inside, but I don't have a key to the kirk."

McLaren and Sue went back to their hotel room and made a list of cemetery addresses they found in the phone book. They spent the day looking through cemeteries, and found two Patersons, but both had lady names. They attended Tiny Kirk the next day, Sunday, and talked to a few people about McLaren's Scottish ancestors, but didn't learn anything.

They ate breakfast early on Monday; Sue took McLaren to the Office Spaces and left him there. He went through a door labeled 'Entrance,' looked for Mr. Barker, and found him in a small room at the end of a long hall. He presented Mr. Barker with the tentative contract he wrote in Rounder. Mr. Barker looked only at the total cost of the proposed contract and replied, "I'm sure it's satisfactory. Where do I sign?"

"I think it's good too, and I hope it is, but let's talk about it and make sure it means the same things to both of us."

Mr. Barker still didn't look seriously at the contract, so McLaren advised him, "The contract describes what I think we should do here, but if you sign it now and change your mind part way through, you could be out more money."

"I won't change my mind. I know nothing about it. You're the expert, and I trust you."

"Thank you, Mr. Barker. Does that mean you don't want me to update you about what I do as I go?"

"That's right. I have plenty to worry about already. I hired you to worry about the grounds."

"OK, go ahead and sign it if you're sure about it, and I'll start work."

"Yeah, fine." Barker signed.

"I'll go outside to make a detailed map of the grounds and will then disappear for a couple days while I work out the plan. I'll see you on Wednesday—or maybe I won't. Perhaps I should just say I'll be back Wednesday?"

"Right."

McLaren almost finished his mapping work before Sue returned. She waited until he did, then she continued as driver. "This road goes west past the firth. I drove all the way past, and I envy your ancestors if they lived anywhere along here. But I also drove around in Inverness and found a wonderful steak house that overlooks a river and a canal, landscaped so beautifully I wonder if you did it." She smiled.

"Are you suggesting we eat there tonight?"

"You're really quick, McLaren. Let's do."

During supper McLaren wondered, "Do you think you should telephone Celeste this evening and see how Skip's doing?"

"Evening here is middle of the day there, remember? Celeste's at work now."

"Right. I wonder if Tim knows about Skip?"

"He might, but he won't be in the house. Do you suppose your Momma knows?"

"I doubt it. It might be good to touch base, though. You want to call her, or should I?"

"Why don't you? She'll appreciate it more if you do it."

McLaren called that evening, and discovered Celeste claimed Skip 'made progress,' but Rose didn't know more.

McLaren worked on the Office Spaces project most of the summer, and presented it as a finished work in August. "Great job, Mr. Paterson. I watched it take shape all summer long, and it's great. I especially like those tall trees you put in front. The building looks a bit shabby, but I think everybody'll look at the trees instead of the building. You're worth every pound of the cost to bring you from abroad, and if anybody asks, I'll tell'em. We have a ceremony on tap to dedicate the new look, a week from tomorrow, and we expect you to speak."

"I'm sorry, Mr. Barker. We have plane tickets for Monday, the day before, so we can't be here."

"You have to change your tickets to Wednesday, because the programs are already printed and show you as the main speaker."

"How come I didn't know about this until now?"

"I apologize. I fear I'm not very organized."

"I'll try to accommodate you Mr. Barker, but I gotta talk to my wife before I can agree."

"If you have trouble with her call me, because we don't have a backup plan."

He had the car that day and drove it back to the hotel to talk to Sue. She responded, "Wonderful McLaren. That will give us two more days to enjoy this beautiful area. We've gone every direction from Inverness except north, so why don't we drive around on the north side?"

"There's only water up there, Sue, no roads. We can't drive there."

"I don't mean straight north, but we can look around on the northeast. We don't want to miss it if it's as beautiful as the other directions, especially since we have time."

"Perhaps, but I need to think sometime about what I'll say on Tuesday."

"I know you. You're thinking about it already. You'll have it so clear in your mind by Tuesday that a day of inactivity will make you nervous."

"You have me figured out, don't you?"

"You couldn't keep a secret from me if you tried, McLaren."

"OK, we can drive up there. But I need to call Barker and tell him we'll stay. Then we must call Momma and tell her we'll be two days late." They enjoyed the Monday drive, and although McLaren later told Sue he didn't do his best work on the Tuesday speech, he thought he did a decent job.

They arrived in Kansas City on Friday evening, August 20, before Sue's classes began. They went out to the farm Saturday and Rose met them at the door. "You'll never guess what Skip and Cindy are up to."

Chapter 24
1965

McLaren tried to guess what Rose hinted. "What are they up to? They're reading, right?"

Rose grinned and replied, "Yes, but they're dating, too. Celeste says it's serious."

McLaren laughed. "Momma, you're an incurable gossip."

"You may think it's only gossip, but I believe it."

"Be that as it may, Momma, have you heard anything about Skip's reading progress?"

"Celeste says he's doing great."

"Great as in ready for college?"

"I don't know about that, McLaren. Celeste says 'great' and that's all I know."

"Are Poppa and Tim in the house?"

"No. I expect them for lunch, but not for a while."

"Do you know where they are?"

"I think they went over west someplace McLaren, but I could be wrong."

Sue and McLaren sat in the kitchen while Rose worked. They told her about Inverness and it's beauty, but admitted they didn't learn about Patersons in the area. They talked an hour or so, and went back to Rounder without seeing Laren and Tim.

They entered their apartment and Sue asked, "Do you think it's wrong to call Celeste and ask her about Skip and Cindy?"

McLaren guffawed. "Sue, you're as bad as Momma. If they want to date, that's their business, not ours."

"Perhaps you're right." She paused. "I think I'll telephone Celeste anyway, and tell her we're back. I won't ask about Skip and Cindy."

"But let me guess. If Celeste talks about them, you won't hang up, right?"

Sue laughed. "I can't keep a secret from you, either, can I?"

"I can read you like a book, Sue."

"OK, I won't call Celeste. Maybe she'll call me."

Celeste didn't call, but McLaren and Sue noticed Skip and Cindy attended Rounder Church on Sunday, and they sat together.

Celeste talked mostly about Skip and Cindy at Rose's Sunday dinner. "Cindy says Skip reads at the eighth grade level, but courts at the college graduate level. He's the first man she's liked, and she thinks they might be in love. She says she always felt sorry for pastor's wives, but if the pastor is Skip, maybe it won't be so bad."

McLaren responded, "Celeste, I'm profoundly uninterested in how Skip courts, but I'm worried about the eighth grade reading level. Should he hold off on college until he reads better?"

"Cindy says a lot of college students today read at that level. She says he'll be fine."

"How does she know a lot of college people read at the eighth grade level?"

"She doesn't say how, McLaren, she merely says it."

"Did she tell you if Skip's improving—with his reading that is?"

"Yes, she said he's at eighth grade level now, up from sixth grade about three weeks ago."

"Do you know if he found a scholarship this summer?"

"I don't know, McLaren, but Cindy says he doesn't need one. She says her expenses are low and she can help him."

McLaren and Sue stayed and talked almost three hours after dinner, then went home. McLaren wondered, "Do you think we should check in with Skip, tell him we're back, and ask if he needs anything?"

"You laughed at me yesterday when I wanted to call Celeste."

"This is different, Sue."

"Really?"

"Yes. The purpose is different. You wanted to learn juicy gossip. I want to learn about his reading."

"Really? Shall we call, or go over?"

McLaren looked at his watch. "How about go over?"

"I'm ready, but Cindy's probably visiting now. Do you want to talk to Skip with her there?"

"You're probably right about Cindy. And no, I'd rather talk to Skip alone. Perhaps I can call and make an appointment for early tomorrow when Cindy might not be there."

"I can go as early as he wants."

"He might be more willing to talk if I go alone, Sue."

Sue sniffed, "I don't know what's wrong with me, but if you prefer to go by yourself, I'll stay home."

McLaren called Skip and received permission to visit at 6:30 Monday morning. Skip smiled when McLaren arrived. "Come in. You're lookin' healthy. Maybe Scotland agrees with you."

"Yeah, Scotland's great. We did some work and had fun too. I hope you can say the same."

"I sure can, McLaren. The readin's a comin' along, but I may drop it and get married."

McLaren smiled and slapped Skip on the back. "The 'get married' part sounds great Skip. Is it connected to the 'drop reading' part?"

"Yeah, it is. Cindy has a good job. I can work some at the gas station, work around the house, and she can support us."

"Does that mean you no longer feel called to be a pastor?"

"It about has to if I drop out of college, don't it?"

"How's Cindy feel about all that?"

Skip answered without conviction. "She's OK with it."

"Is it possible to be married and be ambitious at the same time?"

"Maybe. But it don't seem necessary."

"It might not be necessary from a survival standpoint. But what about from a self-esteem standpoint?"

"You tryin' to tell me what to do?"

McLaren was quiet a moment before he answered. "My brother, Baird, talked to me about my plans a long time ago. He talked to me as a brother, not as somebody trying to tell me what to do. I didn't agree with him straight away, but after he talked to me, he backed off and let me decide on my own. Can I do that with you?"

"Sure, McLaren, shoot."

"Did something happen in past months to make you doubt your call to preach?"

"Cindy."

"Do you think Cindy will respect you in coming years if you quit on her?"

"I ain't aimin' on quittin'. I'm just gonna slow down some."

"Your slowdown may turn into a quit even if you don't intend it. Baird told me money's not the important thing, but you won't get rich if you work in a gas station *or* a church. So if you're not after money, then maybe a challenge? Will you always be content to work in a gas station, or will you perhaps someday wish you'd tried for a bigger challenge? You need to pray about it, and then it's your decision to make, Skip. I hope you don't let your life almost pass you by, then have to run twice as fast to catch up. Sue's offer to give you a ride to Jakesville still stands. Are you enrolled down there?"

"Yeah, I'm enrolled, but Cindy'll save money if I don't show up, and I'll have an easier time."

"Let us know if you want that ride with Sue."

"Thanks, McLaren. I'll think about what you say, I really will. I'll talk about it with Cindy, too."

McLaren went home and told Sue what happened. He added, "We're still praying about Skip's foot, but we need to pray he'll make the right decision, too."

Sue grinned. "And you know exactly what that right decision is, don't you?"

McLaren grinned too. "I thought I did, but you make me realize maybe I don't."

"In any case, you're right, we need to pray." They prayed.

The Paterson telephone rang on Tuesday afternoon and McLaren answered.

"This is Thomas Cartwright of Civic Organization Limited in Inverness. I'm authorized to ask you to come to speak in an outdoor amphitheater next year. The occasion is the founding anniversary of our organization, and our mission for 1966 is to foster grounds beautification in the Scottish Highlands. The date is Saturday, April 9, and we can pay a handsome stipend. What do you say?"

"I'm afraid I'm undecided, Mr. Cartwright. May I call you tomorrow at this time with a decision?"

"We'd be happier with a quick yes, but we can wait if you want to take only a day."

"Thank you, Mr. Cartwright. Good bye."

Sue inquired, "Who was that?"

"A Mr. Cartwright in Inverness; he wants a speech in April. I'm not up for a return to Inverness, especially since you can't go then. I soared all summer this year, but maybe the groundhog work piled up and I should give more attention to Skip, Tim, and Poppa next year."

"Since I can't go—and I can't, because of college—I shouldn't influence you about whether you go."

"McLaren grinned. "Go ahead and influence me. Do you think you can?"

Sue laughed an impish laugh. "What if I say 'go, stay, go, stay?' What will you do?"

"You're no help, Sue. Isn't there someplace you need to be, like all the way across town?"

Sue laughed again. "How about if I come and sit on your lap?"

"Do it. That'll wreck my decider, but do it." She did it, and McLaren giggled. "I'll never decide anything—and I don't think you care—I don't care, that's for sure."

Sue tickled him, wriggled around a bit, and went back to her chair. "I'll let you think now."

"Think? How can I think? Should I think about something?"

"Perhaps about whether to go to Inverness?"

"I don't need to think about that. I won't go, because I'll miss too much time with you. I'm not sure I wanta go around the block right now."

"Oh, McLaren, I didn't try to tell you not to go."

"You didn't have to, because I don't want to go anyway. My decision should balance what I want to do with what will bring in cash. We don't need cash, so the decision's obvious; I wonder if my thinking in any way parallels Skip's?"

"No, it's a different thing, McLaren."

"I think so, but Skip might not."

"Skip doesn't even know your thinking."

"No, but you know what I mean."

"Yes, I know."

McLaren called Mr. Cartwright the next day and declined the job. He suggested a professor of horticulture at a university in the UK, and never learned the outcome.

Chapter 25
1965

McLaren turned down the trip to Inverness, but told Sue he'd take a speaking job closer to home. When the telephone rang on Wednesday afternoon, however, the caller didn't invite him to speak. Sue answered, handed the receiver to him, and said, "It's for you."

"This is Tim. Mrs. Paterson asked me to call. Can you come out to the farm fast?"

"Yes, Tim, is something wrong?"

"It's Mr. Paterson. He passed out and drove the tractor through a fence. We think he's all right now, but Mrs. Paterson's worried."

"I'll be there as fast as I can, Tim."

McLaren slammed the phone down and headed for the door. "I gotta go, Sue. It's Poppa."

"Is he sick?"

"I don't know. I gotta go." McLaren ran out the door as he said it.

"I'll go too." She chased him outside and jumped in the car beside him.

They set a personal speed record and arrived at the farm quickly. Laren sat in a chair outside under a shade tree, Tim stood behind him looking glum, and Rose stood in front of him waving a fan. McLaren jumped out of the car and ran toward the chair. "You all right Poppa?"

McLaren never saw Laren's face so pale in summer, but he spoke with a steady voice. "I'm fine. I don't know why all the fuss."

"Did you see what happened, Tim?"

"Yes, I worked in the fencerow, cutting thistles."

"What happened?"

"He drove the tractor toward the fence, and didn't turn. He went through it and stopped when the back tire hit a tree. He couldn't walk or talk at first, but didn't fall off the tractor, and came out of it enough I could help him walk home."

McLaren asked Rose, "What do you think we should do Momma?"

"I don't know, and that's why I had Tim call you. Laren never did this before; something's wrong."

"We must take him to the hospital at Jakesville. Can you walk to the car, Poppa?"

Laren snorted and frowned. "Of course." He tried to stand, but fell back in the chair. "Maybe I can use a little help."

McLaren and Tim helped Laren to the front seat of Sue's car. Rose, Tim, and Sue got in back, and McLaren drove like a wild man until they arrived at the hospital. Tim and McLaren prepared to help Laren into the emergency room, but he insisted he walk on his own. He sat about a half hour before a doctor saw him, then Tim explained what happened all over again. The doctor listened to Laren's heart and lungs. "I can't hear evidence of anything now, but I'd like to keep him overnight for observation. It might have been a minor stroke or heart attack. If something big's about to happen, we want it to happen here in the hospital."

Rose quickly replied, "Whatever you think, Doctor. We want him home, but only after you say he's all right."

Laren protested, but was overruled four to one. His family didn't leave immediately, but waited until he moved to a room and a bed. Rose decided at the last minute to stay all night, so McLaren, Sue, and Tim went back to the farm. McLaren spoke to Tim, "I've not helped with chores for so long you probably think I don't remember anything about it, but I do. Do you want help?"

"I don't need help McLaren, but will you stay and talk to me?"

"Absolutely anything you want, Tim. I can't tell you how glad I am you helped Poppa when he did whatever he did." McLaren stayed with

Tim all through the chores, then asked, "What can you do with this milk, hot as it is?"

"Can you use it?"

"Not all of it. Maybe Sue can give some of it away. Will you be all right out here by yourself tonight?"

"I feel like a chicken, McLaren, but I've never been here by myself at night before. Can I come to Rounder and stay with you-all?"

"You absolutely can, Tim. You need anything out of the house?"

"Not if you can bring me out here after breakfast tomorrow. I have to do the morning chores."

"I'll bring you out and help you, then you can go with Sue and me to check on Poppa. I hope he'll be fine and can come home. I'll holler at Sue and we'll go if you don't need anything."

Tim and the Patersons went to Rounder that evening, then back out to the farm after breakfast to do chores the next morning. McLaren suggested Tim pour most of the morning's milk on the chickens' feed, and take only a half a bucketful in the house. They went from the farm to Jakesville, and worried about what they'd find there. Rose bubbled and smiled when they entered Laren's room, but then she fretted also. She said he had a good night but couldn't leave until the doctor came to formally release him. They waited a good two hours before the doctor showed up, listened with his stethoscope again, and then spoke to Rose. "I still don't hear anything amiss. Something happened, but I can't say for sure what." The doctor turned to Laren. "I'll dismiss you, but I want you to go slow until the weather cools. Don't get too hot and don't get winded or tired. If any of that happens, you get right back down here, you understand? I want to see you here in about a month. How about September 24?"

Laren agreed to the date, the doctor dismissed him, and everybody except the doctor went back to the farm. McLaren talked sternly to Laren there. "You don't have to do much of anything. If heavy work comes up, let Tim do it or save it for Tim and me. I'll be out every day to check on you for at least a month, and I wanta find you in that chair under the shade tree almost every time. Remember, most work, and heavy work especially, is for Tim and me."

Laren grinned through most of McLaren's lecture, shook his head, and said, "You forget who's the Poppa here, whose farm this is, and who's in charge here."

Rose stomped her foot and screamed, "I'm in charge here, and you'll do what McLaren says."

Laren nodded meekly, but blustered, "I might do something now and then on your say-so, Rose, but not on anybody else's."

McLaren and Sue stood around and talked a few minutes, then went back to Rounder. McLaren commented, "It's good I didn't plan to go to Inverness. If I did, I'd have to plan differently now. I wanted to talk all over the US this fall, but now I'll say no to any offer that will keep me away overnight. Luckily, people aren't exactly beating our door down about that."

Sue grinned. "Maybe you'll be stuck here with me, all fall."

McLaren didn't grin, but agreed. "Yes, you and Poppa. I hope he's OK, but even if he is, Momma needs a lot of support."

Sue sobered. "Yes, you're right. I feel like a slacker, merely going to school. You have the heavy load."

"Speaking of school, did Skip ever call and want to ride with you?"

"Not so far, McLaren."

"I hope he will, but I don't think it'll help to bug him about it."

McClaren went alone to the farm the next day, Friday, and found no problem. He and Tim did the chores, he returned to Rounder, and found a grinning Sue. "Skip called after you left. He asked to ride to Jakesville to college with me. So we compared class schedules and worked out a commuting schedule. You persuaded him when you talked with him."

"I don't know if he decided because of anything I said, but I agree, I think he decided right."

"Everybody's all right at the farm, I guess?"

"As nearly as I can tell. Tim's responsible for a lot out there and I know it's a load for a fourteen-year-old. I'm really glad he's there and as grown-up as he is. If I couldn't count on him to be the groundhog, my eagle days would've ended long ago, I'm afraid."

"Yes, Tim's been through a lot. He never had anybody stable in his life, except his mom, until he moved in with your parents. If he's not grateful, he should be."

"We should be grateful to him too, and I for one, am. Your school starts next week, right?"

"Right. It does."

"So I have to carry on by myself here?"

"Looks like it, but don't look so abused. I know you can do it." She laughed.

Sue returned to college, along with Skip. Although Skip continued to improve, he couldn't read fast enough to cover as much as his teachers assigned. A large group of people promised earlier to read to him when he fell behind, but Cindy did it all.

Laren had a successful September appointment with the doctor. The doctor still could find nothing wrong and released him to ease back into a normal life, but urged him to be cautious and to avoid working alone.

Chapter 26
1965

Skip studied diligently and earned a B-minus average his first semester. He smiled all through a discussion of it. "McLaren, I'm sorry I gave you grief about a college education. I know a semester ain't the whole thing, but I had no idea it depends on me—on the student— so much. I thought your degree fell on you in a lucky accident. Now I know, even though it's work, anybody can do it. I'm a lot less impressed with you, now that I see even I can do it!"

McLaren laughed. "Yes, and the further into college you go, the less impressed you'll be." He laughed too.

A request for a speech in Nashville came in September, and for another in Denver in October, but McLaren turned down both. Christmas came on Saturday in 1965. Baird, Maye and Elizabeth came from Boston, but Joseph couldn't get out of basic training at Fort Sill. Everybody stayed until chore time, when Baird and his family started late for Boston, McLaren went outside with Laren and Tim, and Sue stayed inside to visit longer with Rose.

McLaren and Sue went back to Rounder when the men finished chores. They went on their honeymoon the year before, but planned a mini-repeat of it, and had plane tickets to depart Kansas City on Monday, the twenty-seventh. They didn't use them.

They planned to fly out at 11:10 am Monday, and set their alarm for early Monday, but awakened to freezing rain with a thick layer of ice already on the ground. McLaren looked out and scowled. "Normally, I'd wanta start early today. Traffic's slow for sure."

"What do you mean 'normally'?"

"Poppa acts OK now, but I don't wanta be away from home if he has extra work due to bad weather."

"Tim's out there. I think Poppa's fine, but I'm not so sure about the roads. Should we even try it?"

"I hope you're right about Poppa. We need to start early if we go, but we've traveled in worse."

"I think we'll enjoy staying snug and warm right here in our own apartment more than we will sliding around on ice. Why don't we forget Florida and try again next year?"

"Conditions're bad now, but the rain stopped, so roads'll improve, and maybe it won't be completely terrible for Poppa."

Sue turned the radio on, learned multiple accidents stopped traffic all across Kansas City, and officials closed the airport. She informed McLaren, and added, "The impossible doesn't make sense. We need to stay home."

"No, they'll reopen the airport before we get there. I worry more about Poppa, but maybe we can check in by phone every day. As for us, we merely have to leave earlier than we planned." McLaren used his 'I'm talking to a small child' voice as he said it. They left the apartment early, but before they entered the on-ramp to the highway west out of Rounder, noticed cars stopped as far as they could see. McLaren pulled over on the shoulder, short of the on-ramp. "Let's wait here a minute until they move again."

"I told you, McLaren, the radio says it's this way all over Kansas City. We could go part way, get caught in something like that," Sue pointed ahead, "and not be able to go on or come back. We need to go back home."

They waited by the on-ramp for several minutes before McLaren agreed with her, and they came back to the apartment. Sue made hot chocolate, she talked an hour to Celeste on the phone, McLaren looked at a horticulture book, they played Monopoly, and they generally lazed all day. McLaren looked out the window for the umpteenth time during the afternoon and commented, "Rain stopped for a while, but it's falling again. We may be stuck here tomorrow, too."

Sue replied, "I'll call Cindy. Perhaps she and Skip can come over tomorrow, and we can play Yahtzee, or something." She didn't get an answer to her first call, but found Cindy at Skip's on her second.

Cindy reported Skip would be off work at four o'clock on Tuesday, and she predicted they'd come over soon after. Sue replied, "That's wonderful Cindy. I'll prepare a light supper and you can stay through the evening."

"I have to talk to Skip, but I'll love it, and he probably will too."

Sue told McLaren what happened and made him suspicious. "Why's Cindy at Skip's rooming house when Skip's at work?"

"I don't know, but to use an oft-repeated McLarenism, it's none of our business. We have hot dogs and buns I can use tomorrow evening, and I'll make hot chocolate again for later. Can you walk to the grocery store for chips?"

McLaren grumbled before he went out in the rain, but he went. The rain stopped again during the night on Monday, but roads remained a mess on Tuesday, and the Patersons stayed in their apartment again. Skip and Cindy arrived a tad early; Sue heated the hotdogs and served them first thing. She had the Yahtzee board ready in the living room, but everyone remained in the kitchen, because Skip announced, "Cindy and I are engaged. We plan to marry in March, so I'll lay out of college this coming semester. I'll—"

Cindy turned toward Sue. "We argued about that. I'm afraid if he drops out for a semester he'll never go back. Can you talk some sense into him?"

McLaren opened his mouth, but Sue cut him off. "We wouldn't interfere in your decisions in a thousand years. I'm pretty well acquainted with Skip because of our commutes, and I know he has a level head on his shoulders. We'll leave that for you two to decide. Shall we go in the next room and play Yahtzee?"

No one moved. Skip argued, "Cindy thinks I won't go back, but I will. I just think getting married is all we can handle for now. Cindy don't know how tough college is."

Cindy leaned forward, raised her voice and ranted, "I don't know how tough college is? I don't know how   which of us has the college degree, Skip? Answer me that. I won't sit here and listen to this any more." Cindy stood up, stormed out the door, and drove away.

Skip muttered, "Maybe I should go too."

McLaren pulled on Skip's arm. "Wait, Skip. You wanta talk?"

"I do, but to Cindy. I hope the wedding ain't off."

Sue worried, "Do you know where Cindy might go, Skip? She took her car."

"Yeah, I bet she went over to Celeste's. That's only a couple o' blocks."

McLaren suggested, "Do you think you ought to stay here a few minutes and let her cool off?"

"No, she and Celeste egg each other on. I should get over there before it happens. Bye." Skip burst out the door and tried to run down the icy street toward Celeste's apartment.

McLaren and Sue stood by their open door and watched for a moment. McLaren closed the door and asked, "What do you make of that?"

"I think we both want Skip to stay in school, but I'd rather he drop out than break up with Cindy. I don't know what to think. He might have pushed her farther than she'll go. I wish I hadn't invited them."

"It's not your fault, Sue. They have a big problem, but it's theirs. The only thing we can do about it is pray and leave it in God's hands. Our own hands aren't up to it."

"Do you mean we should sit here and do nothing?"

"What can we do?"

"There's surely something, McLaren."

"Yeah, there are a lot of things. Do you know any that won't make matters worse?"

Sue didn't talk for a moment, then murmured weakly, "No." After another pause, she asked, "Do you think I should call Celeste to see if it's better?"

"No, Sue, no, no, no. The best we can do about their problem is stay out of it. If we do nothing more than give advice, we'll please one and antagonize the other. We can pray, and that's all."

"Did you ever hear the phrase, 'put feet to your prayer'?"

"It's a good-sounding phrase, but where'll you put the feet, Sue?"

"Perhaps if we pray, God will tell us."

"Maybe, but until He does, we need to stay out of it."

Sue and McLaren didn't sleep soundly on Tuesday night, but McLaren looked out a window on Wednesday morning and announced, "Rain's stopped and water's dripping. Maybe ice'll melt today."

"I hope so McLaren. Maybe if Cindy and Skip go out in the cool air they'll make up."

"Will you quit worrying about those two? We need to do something a little more interesting than sleep and watch people fight today. You have any ideas?"

"Not really, McLaren."

"I'm stir crazy. We gotta think of something."

Chapter 27
1965

McLaren's boredom looked unending; Wednesday began on the same dull note as Tuesday, but the telephone rang about 9:30. Sue wondered, "Who can that be?" She answered, "Hello?"

Rose asked, "Can you and McLaren come out here right away?"

"Oh, no—I mean, yes. Is everybody all right?"

"Yes, we're all OK. Laren wants to ask McLaren's advice."

"The roads are bad, but we'll be there as soon as we can. What's Laren's question?"

"He wants to tell you himself. How soon do you expect to be here?"

"We'll leave as soon as we put our coats on. We'll be right out." Sue hung up the telephone, informed McLaren, and they drove to the farm. A pickup truck with lettering on the side blocked the east driveway when they arrived, so they parked across the road in the west drive, hurried back across the road, and entered the house. A man McLaren didn't know stood in the kitchen, while Rose and Laren sat. McLaren glanced from Laren to Rose and back again. "What's goin' on here?"

Laren answered with an introduction. "This is Kenny Benson of Oil Drillers, Inc. Kenny, this is my son McLaren and his wife Sue."

McLaren questioned, "Yes?"

Rose responded, "Mr. Benson wants to look for oil on our farm, and we want your advice."

McLaren paused, looked out the window, and asked, "Can you tell us more?"

Mr. Benson took over the conversation. "Yes, I can. We found oil in Missouri over by the Kansas state line, and we want to look here. We figure there's a fifty-fifty chance we can drill wells to produce around eight hundred barrels a month. If it happens, it will be huge. Oil's worth around two dollars a barrel, and your parents' share will be twelve per cent, so they'll realize close to two hundred a month on a well producing that much."

McLaren responded, "Forgive me for being skeptical, Mr. Benson, but you said a fifty-fifty chance?"

"Right. Or maybe a little less."

"So you probably won't find anything, they'll be left with a hole in the ground, a tracked-up pasture, and will have nothing to show for it?"

"That's up to them. We offer full participation in the risk and potential reward, or we offer no participation in the risk part. We plan to drill two holes over here on this side of the road, and if we find oil, then three more across the road. If your parents decide they want no risk, we'll pay a total of $8,000 per well up front, and take all the oil. Or they can split it up—take the risk on some wells and not on others."

"Make it clear for us, Mr. Benson. I understand the full participation part, so can they do that west of the road, but receive $16,000 up front on the east side?"

"Yes and no, Mr. Paterson. If we drill on the west side, they can decide before we do. If we don't drill there, we'll offer nothing."

"I think I understand." McLaren looked at each individual in the group, including Tim. "How about you?"

When he received no response, he asked Mr. Benson, "May we talk about it privately and call you in a few days?"

"Sure, if a few days means one day." Mr. Benson grinned. "I'll go and let you talk about it. Here's my card, and be sure to call me tomorrow." He went out the door, started his pickup truck, and drove toward Rounder.

McLaren asked his parents, "Which way are you leaning?"

Laren answered, "That's why we asked you to come out, Son. It's almost too much for us to take in so fast."

"The decision matters, and I don't want to make it. Do we need to review your options?"

"No, Son, we understand those—right Rose?—but we don't know which are best."

"We might think about the consequences of the various decisions, Poppa. Let's say they don't find oil over here. As I understand it, then they're done with both sides of the road, right?"

"Right, Son."

"So you could have $16,000 up front if you choose that, or nothing if you don't, right?"

"Yes, that's what the man said."

"Let's say they do find oil over here. Then you could have $16,000 up front for here, plus $24,000 up front for over west. Or if they drill 5 wells, and they all make 800 barrels per month, you can have—he said 'close to'—two hundred a month times five wells. That works out to about $10,000 a year, or less, depending on what 'close to' means."

Rose laughed and put her hand to her head. "Those numbers are so much bigger than we usually deal with, how will we ever decide?"

"Well, Momma, you have until tomorrow. Sue and I shouldn't decide, so we'll go back to Rounder, but we'll come back out before dark to see what you think."

Rose frowned and protested, "I worked on a big lunch all morning and have more than the three of us can eat. Won't you eat with us?"

Sue exchanged glances with McLaren, and eventually caved. "Of course. We'll love that." They stayed for lunch but left soon after, and found a ringing telephone when they entered their apartment.

Sue ran to answer the telephone. "Hello."

"Sue? This is Celeste. I'm at work, so can't talk long, but I go on break at 2:30. I'll come out in the parking lot at the furniture factory if you can meet me there. We'll have ten minutes."

"Sure, we can do that Celeste. What's it about?"

"It's about Skip and Cindy, but I need to get back to work." Sue hung up the telephone and told McLaren about the call.

He shook his head. "You say she wants to talk about Skip and Cindy? Why do we want to let her drag us into that again?"

"I told her we'd meet her McLaren. We need to at least hear her out."

"It's already two. We need to start over there shortly. You wanta walk or drive?"

"Let's walk. I need to clear my head, and perhaps the cold air'll help do that."

They walked and met Celeste outside the furniture factory. Celeste almost pounced on Sue. "You must call Cindy. She and Skip busted up, but I think they're about to get together again."

"What's my part in that, Celeste?"

"You have to encourage her. She cried for almost twelve hours straight."

"I can go over and pat her on the back, but I can't tell her to go back to Skip or not to go back."

"Can you just call her and ask if there's anything you can do? I worry about her."

"Do you want to tell us anything more?"

"Isn't that enough?"

"Perhaps. McLaren and I can discuss whether I should call, as we walk back home."

Celeste went inside the factory building and Sue and McLaren returned to their apartment. Sue asked McLaren on the way back, "What do you think?"

"I don't know what to think, Sue. I worry about them too, the same as Celeste, but I'm afraid if we poke our nose into it, we'll stir up more problems than we solve."

"I agree, but Celeste wants me to merely call and ask if I can do anything. Perhaps that won't cause trouble."

"The question won't, but what if Cindy wants you to take her side against Skip?"

"I won't do it."

"Won't that make her mad?"

"Maybe. I think I have to take the risk. I don't want Cindy to feel like I dropped her."

"Dropped her?"

"You know, like I'm shunning her, or don't care about her."

"Call her if you must, but don't forget we promised to see Momma and Poppa again today."

She called. "Cindy, this is Sue. I'm concerned about you, and called to make sure you know I'll back you in whatever you decide, about Skip or about anything else. Is there anything you'd like me to do?"

"Thanks Sue. I appreciate that, but must go. Skip's here, and we're in a serious discussion. Can I call you back in ten minutes?"

"Sure, Cindy, I'll be here."

Sue told McLaren what Cindy said, and McLaren replied, "I wonder what that all means?"

"Maybe we'll find out when Cindy calls."

They waited impatiently for Cindy's call, and it came only eight minutes later. Cindy exclaimed, "We worked it out Sue! Skip will stay in school until summer vacation and we'll postpone our wedding until then. Skip apologized for saying I don't know how hard college is, and I apologized for being defensive about it. I think we're back like we want to be."

"That's wonderful, Cindy. I know McLaren will be thrilled too. We're so happy for you."

After the call, Sue explained, "They got back together on their own. I didn't have to be involved. Skip will stay in college, they'll postpone the wedding, and everybody apologized. What could be finer?"

McLaren laughed. "Us, Sue. We could be sweating on a beach in Florida, instead of sweating personal details we can't decide, for people we can't control."

"Yes but have you thought about the oil? If it all works out, your parents can retire and you'll be the most free eagle of all time. Maybe they'll give the farm to Tim and advise him while he runs it."

"I didn't think about that aspect of it, but you're right. I hope something does work out, but if they decide to take the full risk and there's no oil, then they won't be anything but disappointed."

"That's up to them isn't it?"

"Yes and I'm glad. We can decide something like that for us, but not for them. Do you remember when I told you about the talk I had with Baird about gold?"

"Barely. What was his point?"

"He related food to gold and called food another, more useful form of gold. Oil is also gold in another form. It's black gold, and we all need it. I wonder why I wanted to find the wrong form of gold? Baird told me few people need the gold I wanted to find, but we all need various other forms. I prayed for God to help me decide whether to be an eagle or a groundhog; maybe He put oil under the ground eons ago, so the decision will make itself."

They sat around in their own apartment another hour, then returned to the farm and found everyone inside. Laren began the conversation. "We decided to take the $16,000 up front, and if they hit oil here, we'll take the $24,000 up front for the west side."

McLaren answered, "The first part of that sounds like a good decision to me Poppa. If you pass up the $16,000 you could end up with nothing. But you don't have to decide on the other by tomorrow."

"You're right, but the starting $16,000 allows the drillers to look for oil as surely as if we held out for more, and it's more than enough for us to retire, more than we ever thought we'd have. We think we should accept it, be grateful, and hope they find more oil than they expect. If they offer us a sure $24,000 to drill west of the road, we'll accept that too, even though we don't need it. We don't want to be greedy, or shoot ourselves in the foot trying for an uncertain monstrous pile of cash, when a certain huge pile is already here. Momma and I aren't much for gambling. We've decided."

"Super, Poppa. So you know what you'll tell Mr. Benson tomorrow, and we think you decided exactly right." McLaren beckoned to Sue. "We'll soar back to Rounder now."

Appendix 1. Relevant Names

Patersons:

Erroll/Kenzie Paterson
Laren/Rose Paterson
McLaren Paterson, son of Laren/Rose
Sue Paterson, wife of McLaren
Baird Paterson, son of Laren/Rose
Maye Paterson, wife of Baird
Joseph Paterson, son of Baird/Maye
Elizabeth Paterson, daughter of Baird/Maye

Cecil Anderson	Land seller
Reginald Barker	Manager of NW Medical Office Spaces, UK
Skip Barnes	Pestered McClaren, became a friend
Kenny Benson	Oil Drillers, Inc.
Burt/Thelma Bradley	Befriended Erroll/Kenzie in UK
James Bradley	Befriended Erroll/Kenzie in UK
Thomas Cartwright	UK Civic Club
Ron/Jan Cline	Neighbors
Kenneth and Claude Cline	Sons of Ron/Jan
Christine Crewes	RHS math teacher

Sharon D'Arliss	Rounder Realty
Conrad Decker	Rounder Lawyer
Lance Erskine	Jake County sheriff, 1959
Professor Glaxor	ALU Geology Professor
Miss Mattie Harvey	McLaren's 1-3 grade teacher
Henry	Clothing store owner
Professor Henry	ALU Geology Professor
Cindy Hicks	Celeste's friend
Ben Jones	Neighbor
Cindy King	Cecelia Shier's daughter, married to Bart
Pastor MacIntire	Tiny Kirk, 1912
Eric McCarty	Bad guy in UK
Dal McCarty	Bad guy in UK, son of Eric
Steve McCoy	Jake County sheriff, 1912
Mr./Mrs. Ed McDowell	Befriended Erroll/Kenzie in UK
Rob Mercer	Hauled cattle
Michelle	McLaren's early girlfriend
Emmanuel/Mary Miller	Neighbors
Rose Miller	Daughter of Emmanuel/Mary Miller
Art Neal	Offered job in Kansas City
Mrs. Jesse Orlando	McLaren's 4-8 grade teacher
Pastor Thomas Ray	Rounder Church, 1959
Mr. Rellerburg	ALU English teacher

Darlene Dyer Cox Wilhelm Rodriguez	Kenzie's mother
Charles Roth	Gardener at Tiny Kirk
Deputy Bill Shields	Sheriff's deputy
Cecelia Shier	Sold farm to Patersons
Ed Shier	Cecelia's deceased husband
Celeste/Timmy Simms	Wife and son of Roy
Roy Simms	Bank robber, murderer
Jim Stone	Cecelia's nephew
Pastor Nick Thomas	Rounder Church, 1912
Mr. Ollie Tollivar	RHS science teacher
Pastor Westerson	Tiny Kirk, 1964

Appendix 2

Birthdays: Erroll John Paterson   Sunday, January 12, 1882
          Kenzie Albretta Cox   Tuesday, January 14, 1882
          Laren Kenneth Paterson   Thursday, March 15, 1914
          Rose Miller, wife of Laren 1913
          McClaren Paterson   Thursday, April 22, 1937
          Joseph, son of Baird   October 21, 1946
          Elizabeth, daughter of Baird August 7, 1948

Weddings: Erroll/Kenzie   Tuesday, February 16, 1904
          Laren/Rose   Sunday, April 7, 1935
          Baird/Maye   1945
          McLaren/Sue   April, 1964

Erroll/Kenzie buy farm in Missouri   Friday, June 28, 1912

Patersons arrive in New York   Saturday, July 27, 1912

Patersons reach Rounder   Wednesday, July 31, 1912

Patersons join Rounder Church   Sunday, October 13, 1912

Ben Jones cuts fence   Thursday, November 21, 1912

Darlene arrives in Rounder   December 19, 1912

World War I   July 28, 1914 – November 11, 1918

Darlene dies   January 21, 1922

ANOTHER FORM

Cecelia Shier dies	November 6, 1928
Ron Cline dies	August 17, 1930
Laren graduates from RHS	May, 1932
Kenzie gives sewing business to Mary Miller	1934
Jan Cline's farm sale	Early 1935
Rose/Laren go to Oklahoma for Baird	Spring, 1935
Jan Cline dies	December 21, 1936
Patersons buy 120 acres	1937
Baird graduates from RHS	1938
Rose/Laren buy first car	1938
Baird graduates from ALU	1942
McClaren enters #5	1943
US involvement in WW II	December 7, 1941 – August, 1945
Electricity to the farm	1946
Telephone installed in east house	1947
Korean War	1950 – 1955
Indoor plumbing, propane heat	1952
Erroll dies, age 71	February 3, 1953
Kenzie dies, age 71	July 12, 1953
McClaren graduates from RHS	1955
Viet Nam War	1955 - 1975